P9-DDP-350

MILDRED AT HOME

The Original Mildred Classics

Mildred Keith

Mildred at Roselands

Mildred and Elsie

Mildred's Married Life

Mildred at Home

Mildred's Boys and Girls

Mildred's New Daughter

MILDRED AT HOME

Book Five of
The Original Mildred Classics

MARTHA FINLEY

CUMBERLAND HOUSE
NASHVILLE, TENNESSEE

MILDRED AT HOME
by Martha Finley

Any unique characteristics of this edition:
Copyright (c) 2001 by Cumberland House Publishing, Inc.

Published by Cumberland House Publishing, Inc.,
431 Harding Industrial Drive, Nashville, Tennessee 37211

All rights reserved. Written permission must be secured from the
publisher to use or reproduce any part of this work, except for
brief quotations in critical reviews or articles.

Cover design by Bruce Gore, Gore Studios, Inc.
Photography by Dean Dixon Photography
Hair and Makeup by Calene Rader
Text design by Julie Pitkin

ISBN 1-58182-231-6

Printed in the United States of America
1 2 3 4 5 6 7 8 — 05 04 03 02 01

MILDRED AT HOME

CHAPTER FIRST

A word spoken in due season, how good is it!

—PROVERBS 15:23

"I'M TO BE dressed in white, mammy, with blue sash and ribbons, papa says, and to go back to him as soon as you are done with me."

"Is you, honey? But co'se you is. You mos' never wears nuffin but white when de warm days comes, an' massa can't do widout his darlin' pet, now all de res' am gone."

"No; nor I without him," Elsie said, tears springing to her eyes. "Oh, don't these rooms seem lonely, mammy? Don't you miss Annis?"

"Co'se, honey, co'se I does. But tank de Lord, I'se got my own darlin' chile lef'."

"And I have you and papa left," returned the little girl, smiling through her tears, "and that's a great deal. Papa alone is more than half of all the world to me, and you know I could never do without you, mammy."

"Yo' ole mammy hopes you'll always tink like dat, honey," said Chloe, taking out the articles needed for the little girl's dressing.

"'Pears like ole times come back," she remarked presently, combing a glossy ringlet round her

7

finger, "de ole times befo' we went up Norf and massa got married to Miss Rose."

"Yes. And oh, mammy, papa has said I may be with him all day long, from the time I'm up in the morning and dressed, till I have to go to bed at night. Isn't it nice?"

"Berry nice plan, honey; 'spect it keep bofe you and massa from feelin' mos' pow'ful lonesome."

"Yes," Elsie said, "and I like it ever so much for a little while, but I wouldn't for anything be without mamma and Horace all the time."

Aunt Chloe was still busy with the ringlets. She took almost as much pride and delight in their beauty and abundance as the fond father himself, and she was apt to linger lovingly over her task. But Elsie, though wont to endure with exemplary patience and resignation the somewhat tedious and trying ordeal of combing and curling, never complaining—though now and then compelled to wince when the comb caught in a tangle and mammy gave a pull that was far from pleasant— would sometimes have been glad to have them cut off, would papa only have given consent.

"Dar, honey, dat job am done," Aunt Chloe said at length, laying aside the comb and brush. "Now fo' de dress and ribbons, an' den you kin go back to massa."

"I want to just as soon as I can," said the little girl.

"What goin' be done 'bout pourin' de tea tonight?" asked Aunt Chloe presently, rather as if thinking aloud than speaking to Elsie.

"Why?" queried the little girl. "Won't Mrs. Murray do it as usual?"

"Dunno, chile, she hab a pow'ful bad headache."

"Has she? How sorry I am! Oh, I wonder if papa would let me try!"

"'Spect so, honey, ef you axes him," said Aunt Chloe, giving a final adjustment to the bows of the sash and the folds of the dress.

"So I will," cried the little girl, skipping away. But the next instant, coming to a sudden standstill and turning toward her nurse a face full of concern, she asked, "Mammy, do you think I can do anything to help poor Mrs. Murray's head?"

"No, chile, she ain't wantin' nuffin but to be let 'lone till de sickness am gone."

"I wish I could help her," sighed Elsie in a tenderly pitying tone. "I'm very sorry for her but hope she will be well again tomorrow."

Two gentlemen were sitting on the veranda. Each turned a smiling, affectionate look upon the little girl as she stepped from the open doorway, the one saying, "Well, daughter," the other, "How are you today, my little friend?"

"Quite well, thank you, Mr. Travilla. How are you, sir?" she said, putting her small white hand into the larger, browner one he held out to her.

He kept it for a minute or two while he chatted with her about the cousins who had just left for their Northern home after spending the winter as guests at the Oaks, and of her mamma and baby brother, who were travelling to Philadelphia in their company.

"I daresay the house seems very quiet and rather lonely?" he remarked, inquiringly.

"Yes, sir, especially in my rooms," she said,

glancing round at her father, who was silently listening to their talk. "But papa has promised to let me be with him all the time during the day. So I shall not mind it so much."

"Was not that a rather rash promise, Dinsmore?" asked Mr. Travilla, with mock gravity. "Well, if you tire of her company at any time, we of Ion shall be delighted to have her sent to us."

"Thank you," Mr. Dinsmore said, with a humorous look at his little girl. "I shall certainly send her to you as soon as I tire of her society."

Elsie glanced searchingly into his face, then with a happy laugh ran to him. Putting her arm about his neck, she said, "I'm not the least bit frightened, papa, not at all afraid that you will want to be rid of me. I hope I'm not quite so silly as I was once when Mr. Travilla made me think you might give me away to him."

"But it was only a loan I was asking for this time, my little friend," was Mr. Travilla's pleasant rejoinder.

"Yes, sir, but if you borrow me you'll have to borrow papa too for the same length of time," Elsie said with a merry laugh. "Won't he, papa?"

"I think he cannot have you on any easier terms," Mr. Dinsmore answered, "for I certainly cannot spare you from home while I stay here alone."

"A satisfactory arrangement to me, provided we are allowed to keep you both as long as we wish," Mr. Travilla said, rising as if to take leave.

But an urgent invitation to stay for tea induced him to resume his seat.

Then Elsie proffered her request.

It was granted at once, her father saying with a

pleased look, "I should like to see how well you can fill your mamma's place. And if you show yourself capable, you may do so always in her absence, if you wish."

"Oh, thank you, papa," she cried in delight. "I'll do my very best. But I'm glad there are no strangers to tea tonight to see me make my first attempt. You are a guest, Mr. Travilla, but not a stranger," she added with a bright, winsome look up at him.

"Thank you, my dear," he said. "It would be a grief of heart to me to be looked upon in that light by the little girl whose affection I value so highly."

"You are very kind to say so, sir," she returned with a blush and a smile, "and I believe I'm every bit as fond of you as if you were my uncle. I have often heard papa say that you and he were like brothers, and that would make you my uncle, wouldn't it?"

"Yes," her father said, "and so good and kind an uncle would be something to be thankful for, wouldn't it? Ah," he said, rising and taking her hand, "there is the tea bell. Now for your experiment. Will you walk out with us, Travilla?"

Both gentlemen watched the little girl with loving interest while she went through the duties of her new position with a quiet grace and dignity that filled her father with proud delight and increased the admiration already felt for her by his friend.

On leaving the table they returned to the veranda, where the gentlemen sat conversing, with Elsie between them.

But presently Mr. Dinsmore, hearing that some one from the quarter wished to speak to him, left the other two alone for a while.

"Elsie," Mr. Travilla said softly, taking the little girl's hand in his, "I have something to tell you."

Her only reply was an inquiring look. He went on: "Something which I am sure you will be glad to hear. But first let me ask if you recall a talk we had one morning at Roselands, the first summer after your father and I returned from Europe?"

"You were so kind as to talk to me a good many times, sir," Elsie answered doubtfully.

"This was the morning after your fall from the piano stool. I found you in the garden reading your Bible and crying over it," he said. "And in the talk that followed, you expressed great concern at the discovery that I had no love for the Lord Jesus Christ. A text you quoted—'If any man love not the Lord Jesus Christ, let him be anathema maranatha'—has since come very frequently to my recollection and has troubled my conscience not a little."

Elsie was now listening with intense interest. Mr. Travilla paused for a moment, his face expressing deep emotion, then resumed: "I think God's Holy Spirit has thoroughly convinced me of the exceeding sinfulness of unbelief, of refusing, or neglecting His offered salvation through the atoning blood of His dear Son, refusing to give to the Lord Jesus the poor little return of the best love of my heart for all He has done and suffered in my stead. This is what I had to tell you, my dear little friend. I have found Jesus—have given myself unreservedly to Him, to be His for time and for eternity, and I have been led to do this mainly through your instrumentality."

Tears of joy filled the little girl's eyes. "I am so glad, Mr. Travilla, so very glad!" she exclaimed. "It is the best news I could possibly have heard."

"Thank you, my dear," he said with feeling. "I can now understand your anxiety for my conversion, for I myself am conscious of a yearning desire for the salvation of souls, especially of those of my friends and acquaintances."

"And now you will join the church, won't you, sir?"

"I don't know, Elsie. That is a question of duty I have not yet decided. There are so many of its members who are a disgrace to their profession that I fear I might prove so also. What do you think about it?"

"I'm only a little child, not half so wise as you are, sir," she answered with unaffected modesty.

"Still, I should like to hear your opinion."

After a moment's hesitation and silent thought she lifted a very earnest face to his. "God tells us that He is able to keep us from falling. And don't you think, Mr. Travilla, that it's what the Bible says we should be guided by, and not what somebody else thinks?"

"Yes, that is quite true."

"'To the law and to the testimony: if they speak not according to this word, it is because there is no light in them,'" she quoted.

"You have studied the Bible so much longer than I," he said, "can you tell me where to look for its directions in regard to this matter? Does it really give any?"

"Yes, sir! Oh, yes! Is not joining the church confessing Christ before men, acknowledging Him as our Master, our Lord, our God?"

He nodded assent.

Elsie called to a servant lounging near and sent him for her Bible.

"Can you find the texts you want without a concordance?" Mr. Travilla asked, regarding her with interest as she took the book and opened it.

"I think I can," she answered, turning over the pages; "I have read them so often. Yes, here — Matthew 10:32, 33 — is one: 'Whosoever therefore shall confess me before men, him will I confess also before my Father which is in heaven. But whosoever shall deny me before men, him will I also deny before my Father which is in heaven.'"

She gave him a questioning, pleading look.

"Yes," he said, in a subdued tone, "I think that is to the point. At least if we grant that joining the church is the only way of confessing Christ."

"Oh, don't you see? Don't you think, Mr. Travilla, that if we love Him with all our hearts we will want to confess Him everywhere and in every way that we can? Won't we want everybody to know that we belong to Him, and acknowledge Him as our Master, our Lord, our King?" she exclaimed with eager enthusiasm, her voice taking a tone of earnest entreaty.

"I believe you are right," he said. "That would be the natural effect of such love as we ought to feel — as I am sure you do feel for Him."

"I do love Him, but not half so much as I ought," she answered with a sigh as again she turned over the leaves of the Bible. "I often wonder how it is that my love to Him is so cold compared to His for me. It is as though I gave Him but one little drop in return for a mighty ocean." A tear fell on the page as she spoke.

Then again she read: "'The gift of God is eternal life through Jesus Christ our Lord.' 'The word is nigh thee, even in thy mouth and in thy heart'—that is, the word of faith which we preach; 'that if thou shalt confess with thy mouth the Lord Jesus, and shalt believe in thine heart that God hath raised Him from the dead, thou shalt be saved. For with the heart man believeth unto righteousness; and with the mouth confession is made unto salvation.'"

Looking up at him, "Oh, Mr. Travilla," she said, "shall we refuse to be soldiers at all because there are some traitors in the army? Isn't there all the more need of brave, true men for that very reason? Plenty of them to fight the Lord's battles and conquer His enemies?"

"Yes, but cannot one do that without becoming a member of a church?"

"Wouldn't that be a strange kind of an army where there was not concert of action, but instead every man fought separately in the way that seemed best to himself?" she asked with modest hesitation. "I've read about the armies and battles of our Revolution and other wars, and I don't remember that there was ever a great victory except where a good many men were joined under one leader."

"Very true," he replied thoughtfully.

"And if you love Jesus, Mr. Travilla, how can you help wanting to obey His dying command,

'Do this in remembrance of me'? And that we cannot do unless we are members of some church."

"I should not hesitate, Elsie, if I were but sure of being able to hold out and not disgrace my profession," he said.

Mr. Dinsmore returned to the veranda and sat down again by Elsie's side, just in time to hear his friend's last sentence.

"It is a profession of religion you are speaking of, I presume," he said, half inquiringly. "Well, Travilla, we must be content to take one step at a time as we follow our Leader, to put on the armor and go into battle trusting in the Captain of our salvation to lead us onto final victory. He bids us 'fear not; I will help thee.' 'As thy days, so shall thy strength be.' 'He keepeth the feet of His saints.' 'Who shall separate us from the love of Christ? . . . We are more than conquerors through Him that loved us. For I am persuaded that neither death, nor life, nor angels, nor principalities, nor powers, nor things present, nor things to come, nor height, nor depth, nor any other creature, shall be able to separate us from the love of God which is in Christ Jesus our Lord,' for His chosen, His redeemed ones, are kept by the power of God through faith unto salvation. For 'He is able to keep you from falling.'"

CHAPTER SECOND

This we commanded you, that if any would not work,
neither should he eat.

—2 THESSALONIANS 3:10

MR. TRAVILLA HAD gone, and Mr. Dinsmore and his little daughter sat alone upon the veranda, she upon his knee, his arm about her waist. Some moments had passed without a word spoken by either. Elsie's eyes were downcast, her face full of solemn joy.

"What is my little girl thinking of?" her father asked at length.

"Oh, papa, I am so glad, so happy, so thankful!" she said. And as she looked up into his face, he saw that tears were glistening in her eyes.

"You are seldom other than happy, I think and hope," he responded, softly stroking her hair.

"Yes, very seldom, dear papa. How could anybody be unhappy with so many, many blessings to be thankful for—especially such a dear, kind father to love and take care of me? But I am happier than usual tonight because of the good news Mr. Travilla has told me."

"Ah, what was that?"

"That he has found the Saviour, papa, and that

it was partly through my instrumentality. Isn't it strange that God should have so honored a child like me?"

"Ah, I don't know that it is. 'A little child shall lead them,' the Bible says. 'Out of the mouth of babes and sucklings thou has perfected praise.' God often works by the feeblest instrumentality, that thus all may see that the glory is due to Him alone. I rejoice with you, my darling, for no greater blessing can be ours than that of being permitted to win souls to Christ."

"Yes, papa, but I am so far from being what I ought," she added with unaffected humility, "that I wonder I have not proved a stumbling block instead of a help."

"Give the glory to God," he said.

"Yes, papa, I know it all belongs to Him. Oh, don't you hope Mr. Travilla will be with us next Sabbath?"

"At the Lord's table? I do indeed. It is a precious privilege I have long wished to share with him. It is a means of grace no Christian ought ever to neglect, a command that, as the last and dying one of our blessed Master, we should joyfully obey whenever opportunity is afforded us, yet with the utmost endeavor to be in a proper frame of mind. For 'he that eateth and drinketh unworthily, eateth and drinketh damnation to himself, not discerning the Lord's body.' It is a dreadful sin for any one to sit down to that table without having examined himself of his knowledge to discern the Lord's body, of his faith to feed upon Him, repentance, love, and new obedience. Let us both pray earnestly for grace and help to partake worthily, repenting of every sin, hating and forsaking it, and devoting ourselves anew and unreservedly to the Master's service."

"I will, papa," she said. "And should we not meditate on Jesus while at His table?"

"Yes, He should be the principal theme of our thoughts all through the exercises. We should remember Him—the loveliness of His character, the life He led, the death He died, and all that He has done and suffered for us."

They fell into silent thought again. Elsie was the first to speak. "I wonder where they are now, papa?"

"Who? Our travellers? Well, we cannot tell precisely, but I hope it will not be very long before we shall hear of their safe arrival in Philadelphia."

"That will end the journey for mamma and Horace," she remarked, "but what a long one the others will still have before them! I should think Annis would feel as if she must hurry on as fast as possible till she gets home to her father and mother."

"Very possibly she may, but I know that Dr. Landreth and Mildred intend resting for some days in Philadelphia. So Annis will be obliged to curb her impatience, which the sights of the city will no doubt help her to do."

At that instant Elsie gave a sudden start, asking in an awed, tremulous whisper, "Papa, what is that?" nestling closer to him as she spoke.

It was growing dusk, and a shadowy figure, dimly seen in the waning light, had just emerged from the shadow of a large tree at some distance down the drive. It was now stealing cautiously in their direction.

"Don't be alarmed, dearest," Mr. Dinsmore said, tightening his clasp of Elsie's slight form. "I presume it is some runaway whom hunger has forced to show himself." Then, to the figure which continued to advance with slow, faltering steps, he called, "Halt! Who are you, and what is your business here?"

"I'se Zeke, massa," answered a trembling voice. "I'se come back to wuk an' hopes you won't be hawd on a po' soul wha's repentin' an' pow'ful sorry fo' takin' a holiday widout yo' leave, sah." Mr. Dinsmore made no reply, and the man drew nearer. "I'se pow'ful sorry, massa," he repeated, pausing at the foot of the veranda steps and standing there in a cringing attitude, his rags fluttering in the evening breeze, the remnant of a straw hat in his hand. "Hope yo won't order me no floggin'."

"If you choose to go back where you came from, I shall not interfere with you, Zeke," returned Mr. Dinsmore, coolly.

"I'se done tired o' de swamp, sah. I'se like to starve to deff dar. Hain't tasted not de fust mawsel o' victuals fo' de las' two days."

"Oh, poor fellow, how hungry he must be!" exclaimed Elsie. "Papa, won't you please give him something to eat?"

"He won't work, Elsie. Since I have known him he has never earned his salt."

"But, papa," she pleaded, "wouldn't it be wrong and cruel to let him starve while we have plenty and to spare?"

"Would it? God's command is, 'Six days shalt thou labor and do all thy work.' And Paul says to the Thessalonians, 'Even when we were with you, this we commanded you, that if any would not work, neither should he eat.'"

Elsie turned to the suppliant. "Zeke, you hear what the Bible says, and you know we must obey all its teachings."

"Yes, Miss Elsie, dat's true nuff."

"Then will you promise papa that if he feeds you now, you will go to work industriously tomorrow, if God spares your life?"

"Sho'n I will, Miss Elsie, 'cept I gets de misery in de back, or de head, or somewheres else."

"He can always find a hole to creep out at, Elsie," Mr. Dinsmore said with a slight laugh. "Those miseries never elude a determined search."

"But, Zeke," said Elsie, "you mustn't give up for a little misery. You mustn't try to feel one."

"Sho' not. But dey jes' comes dereselves, little missy."

"And some people give them every encouragement, while others work on in spite of them," remarked his master with some sternness of tone. "I assure you, Zeke, that I have myself done many an hour's work while enduring a racking headache."

"You, sah? T'ought you didn't never do no wuk."

"Just because you never saw me take hold of spade or hoe? One may toil far harder with the mind, Zeke. Well, I will give you one more trial. Go to the kitchen and tell Aunt Dinah, from me, that she is to give you something to eat. And tomorrow you must go to work with the rest in

21

the field or—starve. And mind, if you have been without food as long as you say, you mustn't eat nearly so much as you want tonight, or you'll kill yourself."

"Tank you, sah, I 'cepts de conditions." And with a low bow, first to Mr. Dinsmore, then to Elsie, he turned and shambled off in the direction of the kitchen.

"Papa, is he so very lazy?" asked Elsie.

"Very. He would do nothing but lie in the sun if allowed to follow his own pleasure, though he is young, strong, and healthy. He disappeared some days ago, but I permitted no search to be made for him and should have been better pleased had I never seen him again."

"Papa, perhaps he might do better at some other work, in the garden or about the stables."

"Possibly. I think I shall try acting upon your suggestion."

"Oh, thank you, sir," she said. Then after a moment's thoughtful silence: "Papa, we are sitting here doing nothing at all, yet I know you must think it right, else you wouldn't do it, or let me."

"It is right: Neither body nor mind was made capable of incessant exertion. We need intervals of rest and can accomplish more in the end by taking them when needed. Jesus once said to His disciples, 'Come ye yourselves apart into a desert place, and rest a while.'"

"Oh, yes! I remember it now," she said. "How good and kind, how thoughtful for others, He always was! Papa, I do so want to be like Him."

"I think you are, my darling," he answered in moved tones, and pressing her closer to him, added, "like Him in sufficient measure for those who know you in your daily life to 'take knowledge of you that you have been with Jesus' and learned of Him."

"Papa, you couldn't say sweeter words to me," she whispered, with her arm about his neck, and he felt a tear fall on his cheek. "And you, papa, oh, I am sure no one could be long in your company without feeling sure that you were one of Jesus' disciples."

"I hope that is so," he said with feeling; "for, like you, I most earnestly desire to honor Him by my daily walk and conversation and to be always and everywhere recognized as His servant."

Elsie, who had the kindest of hearts, thought of Zeke while her mammy was preparing her for bed that night and again while going through the duties of her morning preparations. That completed, she hastened to her father with a request that Zeke might be set to work in her own little garden.

"Weeding and watering it would be very pleasant, easy work, I am sure," she added. "I like to do it myself."

"I doubt if Zeke would know weeds from flowers," her father said, smiling down into the eager little face.

"But I will show him, papa, if I may."

"You may do just as you please about it," was the indulgent reply. "We will have our reading and prayer together, and then you may send for Zeke and give him his instructions."

"Oh, thank you, papa!" she exclaimed with as sincere joy and gratitude as though she had won some great favor for herself.

Mr. Dinsmore rang for a servant and sent a message to Zeke. He was directed to make himself clean and decent and to come to the veranda for further orders.

He obeyed. Elsie found him waiting there, and taking him to her garden, explained minutely what she wished him to do, calling his attention particularly to the difference between the leaves of the weeds that were to be uprooted and those of some annuals not yet in bloom.

He promised faithfully to attend to her directions and to be industrious.

"Don't you think it's nicer, easier work than what you would have to do in the field?" she asked.

"Ya-as, Miss Elsie," he drawled, "but it's stoopin' all de same, and I'se got de misery in de back."

She gave him a searching look, then said reproachfully, "Oh, Zeke, you don't look the least bit sick, and I can't help being afraid you are really lazy. Remember, God knows all about it and is very much displeased with you, if you are not speaking the truth."

"Sho I'se gwine to wuk anyhow, honey," he answered with a sound between a sigh and a groan as he bent down and pulled up a weed.

"That's right," she said pleasantly as she turned and left him.

An hour later, coming out to see what progress he was making, she found nearly all her beloved annuals plucked up by the roots and lying withering among the weeds in the scorching sun.

"Oh, how could you, Zeke!" she cried, her eyes filling with tears.

"Why, what's de mattah, Miss Elsie?" he asked, gaping at her in open-mouthed wonder not unmixed with apprehension and dismay.

"Matter? You've been pulling up flowers as well as weeds. That is one you have in your fingers."

Zeke dropped it as if it had been a hot coal and stood staring at it where it lay wilting on the hot ground. "Sho, Miss Elsie, I didn't go fo' to do no sech ting," he said plaintively. "T'ought I was doin' 'bout right. Shall I plant 'em agin?"

"No, they wouldn't grow," she said.

"Dis soul's mighty sorry, Miss Elsie. You ain't gwine to hab him sent back to de wuk in de field, is you?" he asked with humble entreaty.

"I'm afraid that is all you are fit for, Zeke, but the decision rests with papa. I will go and speak to him about it. Don't try to do any more work here, lest you do more mischief," she said, turning toward the house.

He hurried after her. "Please now, Miss Elsie, don't go for to 'suade massa agin dis po' slave."

"No, I shall not," she answered kindly. "Perhaps there is something else you can be set at about the house or grounds. But, Zeke," she said, turning to him and speaking very earnestly, "you will never succeed at anything unless you strive against your natural laziness and try to do your best. That is what God bids us all do. He says, 'Whatsoever thy hand findeth to do, do it with thy might.' 'Whatsoever ye do, do it heartily, as to the Lord and not unto men.'"

"'Spect dat's so, Miss Elsie," he drawled; "but de Lawd, He ain't gwine to take no notice what a po' slave's 'bout in de field or de garden."

"That's a great mistake, Zeke," she said. "His eye is always on you—on everybody. And He is pleased with us if He sees us trying to do faithfully the work He has given us, no matter how low the task may seem to us or other human creatures, and displeased if we are not trying to do it 'as to the Lord and not unto men.'"

"You ain't 'fended 'bout dose po' flowahs what dis po' slave bin pull up in a mistake, is you now, Miss Elsie?" he asked.

Evidently her religious teachings had made no more impression than the whistling of the wind.

"No, Zeke, I only can't trust you again," she said, turning away with a slight sigh over her failure to win him from his inborn indolence.

She hastened to her father with the story of what had occurred.

"Ah! It is about what I had expected," he said. "I am sorry for your loss, but it can soon be repaired. Have you left Zeke there to finish the work of destruction?"

"No, sir, I told him to stop till he heard from you."

"He shall go back to the field at once. There is no propriety in giving him an opportunity to do further mischief," Mr. Dinsmore said, making a decision that left no room for remonstrance. Summoning a servant, he sent the order.

Elsie heard it with a sigh. "What now? You are not wasting pity on that incorrigibly lazy wretch?" her father asked, drawing her caressingly to his knee.

"I did hope to do him some good, papa," she sighed, "and I'm disappointed that I can't."

"There may be other opportunities in the future," he said. "And do not fret about the flowers. You are welcome to claim all in my gardens and conservatories."

"How good and generous you always are to me, dear father!" she said, thanking him with a hug and kiss while her face grew bright with love and happiness. "No, I won't fret. How wicked it would be for one who has so many blessings! But, papa, I can't help feeling sorry for the little tender plants, plucked up so rudely by the roots and left to perish in the broiling sun. They were live things, and it seems as if they must have felt it all and suffered almost as an insect or an animal would."

Her father smiled and smoothed her hair with softly caressing hand. "My little girl has a very tender heart and is full of loving sympathy for all living things," he said. "Ah, Travilla. Glad to see you!" he said as that gentleman galloped up and dismounted.

"So am I, sir," Elsie said, leaving her father's knee to run with outstretched hand to meet and welcome their guest.

He clasped the little hand in his and held it for a moment while he bent down and kissed the sweet lips of the owner. "What news?" Mr. Dinsmore asked when he had given his friend a seat and resumed his own.

"None that I know of, except that I have come to your view (which is my mother's also) of the subject we were discussing yesterday and have decided to act accordingly," Mr. Travilla answered with a rarely sweet smile directed to little Elsie.

"Oh!" she cried, her face growing radiant, "I am so glad, so very glad!"

"And I, too," said her father. "I am sure you will never regret having come out boldly on the Lord's side."

"No, my only regret will be that I delayed so long enrolling myself among His professed followers. I now feel an ardent desire to be known and recognized as His servant and am ready to go forward, trusting implicitly His many great and precious promises to help me all my journey through."

"'Being confident of this very thing, that He which hath begun a good work in you will perform it until the day of Jesus Christ'?" quoted Mr. Dinsmore inquiringly.

"Yes," said Mr. Travilla, "for He is able to keep that which I have committed unto Him, able to keep even me from falling."

CHAPTER THIRD

AUNT WEALTHY

DR. LANDRETH AND his party reached Philadelphia in due time, arriving in health and safety, having met with no accident or loss on the way.

Mrs. Dinsmore found her father and the family carriage waiting for her and her baby boy at the depot.

The others took a hack and drove to the Girard House, where Miss Stanhope, who had been visiting friends in the neighborhood of the city, had proposed to meet them so that they and she might journey westward together. She was there waiting for them in a private parlor.

The meeting was a joyful one for the two ladies, who, though always warmly attached, had now been separated for a number of years. They clasped each other in a long, tender embrace, then Mildred introduced her husband and exhibited her baby with much pride and delight. Annis, too, for she had quite grown out of Aunt Wealthy's recollection and had scarce any remembrance of the old lady, except from hearing her spoken of by the other members of the family.

The travellers were weary from their journey, and there was much to hear and tell, so the remainder of that day was given up to rest and talk, a part of the latter being on the arrangement of their plans. Mildred proposed that they should take a week or more for rest and shopping, then turn their faces homeward.

"You must allow some time for sightseeing, my dear," said her husband. "It would be a great shame to carry Annis all the way out to Indiana again without having shown her the lions of Philadelphia."

"Oh, certainly she must see them," said Mildred. "You can show them to her while Aunt Wealthy and I are shopping."

"You intend, then, to shut me out of that business? How shall I know that you will not be ruining me?"

"My dear," said Mildred, laughing, "you forget how rich you have made me. I shall have no occasion to ruin anybody but myself."

"And as for me," remarked Miss Stanhope drily, "I have my own purse."

"And father has sent money to buy Ada's things, mother's, and Fan's too," added Annis. "But, Milly, I must have some share in the shopping, too. I expect to enjoy that as much as the sightseeing."

Mildred assured her she should have as much as she wanted, adding, "But there will be a good deal which will not be likely to interest you—napery and other housekeeping goods, for instance."

"Your share of those things will interest me and must be paid for from my purse," put in the doctor.

"Quite a mistake," said Miss Stanhope. "Those are the very things a bride or her parents are expected to supply."

"But Mildred is no longer a bride. Milly, my dear, I want you to help me to select a dress for the bride that is to be."

Mildred looked up with a pleased smile. "That's just like you, Charlie, always thoughtful and generous!"

Ada Keith was the coming bride. She and Frank Osborne had been engaged for some weeks and expected to marry in the fall. This news had increased Annis's desire to get home. She wanted, she said, to see how Mr. Osborne and Ada acted, and whether they looked very happy.

"And just to think" she added, "when they're married, Fan will be Miss Keith, and we two will be the young ladies of the family."

"Ah, indeed! How old may you be, my little maid?" laughed the doctor.

"'Most thirteen," returned the little girl, drawing herself up with an air of importance.

"A very young young lady, most decidedly," he said with a humorous look, bending down to pinch her rosy cheek as he spoke.

"I'm growing older every day," she answered demurely, edging away from him. "Father told me a year ago that I'd soon be a woman."

"Quite soon enough, dear. Don't try to hurry matters," said Aunt Wealthy. "You can never be a little girl again."

Mildred, having brought a competent nurse with her thus far on her journey, a Negro woman who would serve her in the care of little Percy while they remained in Philadelphia and then return to the South with Mrs. Dinsmore, was able to give herself to the shopping without distraction.

As she had foreseen, the greater part of that work fell to her and Miss Stanhope, Dr. Landreth and Annis accompanying them constantly for a day or two only, and after that, for an hour or so when something was to be purchased in which they were specially interested.

But the two ladies were equal to the demand upon them. Mildred had had a good deal of experience in shopping in the last few years, and Miss Stanhope was a veteran at the business—an excellent judge of qualities and prices—yet by reason of her absent-mindedness needed to have her knowledge supplemented by the collected wits of her niece.

The old lady's odd ways and speeches often caused no little amusement to all within sight and hearing.

One day she, her two nieces, and Dr. Landreth were in a large, handsomely appointed dry goods store, looking at silks and other costly dress fabrics.

They had made several selections, and while the doctor and Mildred paid for and saw the goods cut off and put up, Miss Stanhope moved on to the farther end of the room, where she saw, as she thought, an open doorway leading into another of similar dimensions and appearance.

As she attempted to pass through the doorway, she found herself confronted by a little old lady rather plainly attired. Miss Stanhope nodded pleasantly and stepped to the right. At the same instant, her vis-a-vis nodded also and stepped to her left, so that they were still in each other's way. Miss Stanhope moved quickly to the other side, but the stranger doing likewise, and they did not succeed in passing. Miss Stanhope stood still, so did the other, and for an instant they gazed steadily into each other's eyes.

Then Miss Stanhope spoke in a gentle, lady-like, yet slightly impatient tone: "I should like to go on into that part of the store, if you will kindly permit me. Take whichever side you will; or, if you please, stand where you are and let me step past you."

She attempted to do so, but again the stranger moved directly in front of her.

"Madam," said Miss Stanhope, unconsciously raising her voice slightly, "I will stand still if you will be good enough to step out of my way."

There was neither reply nor movement, but Miss Stanhope's ear caught sounds of suppressed laughter coming from various directions behind her, and a clerk, stepping to her side, said, with an unsuccessful attempt to preserve gravity of countenance and steadiness of tone, "Excuse me, madam, but you are standing before a mirror. There is no doorway there."

"Dear me! so I am! What an old simpleton not to recognize my own face!" she exclaimed, joining good naturedly in the laugh her mistake had raised.

"Very good evidence that you are lacking in the vanity that leads some to a frequent contemplation of their own features," remarked the proprietor politely.

"Ah, sir, an old woman like me has small temptation to that," she returned.

"What was it, Aunt Wealthy? What are you all laughing at?" asked Annis, joining her.

"Just at a foolish mistake of your old auntie's, my dear, taking a mirror for an open doorway and her own reflection for another woman who wouldn't get out of her way."

Annis could not help laughing a little, though she tried not to, lest she should hurt the dear old lady's feelings.

"I'm not much surprised, auntie," she said, gazing into the mirror, "for it does seem like looking into another store. I think I might have made that mistake myself, but I never could have taken you for anybody else, and it's odd you didn't know yourself."

"Ah, dearie, self-knowledge is said to be the most rare and difficult thing in the world," returned Miss Stanhope pleasantly. "But come, I see the doctor and Milly are waiting for us."

"We are going to some trimming stores now, Aunt Wealthy," said Mildred, "and you will be able to match your zephyrs, I hope."

"Yes, I'll have my samples out ready to show," the old lady answered, taking them from a small satchel which she carried upon her arm. "You and the doctor walk on. Annis and I will follow. Take tight hold of my arm, dearie," she added, holding it out as they stepped into the street, "lest you should get separated from me and lost in the crowd—the streets are so full, and everybody seems in the greatest hurry."

"Yes," said Annis, doing as she was bidden, "so different from Pleasant Plains. There one can hurry along or not as one likes without being jostled. There! Milly and Brother Charlie have gone into a store, and we must follow."

They hastened in, almost out of breath from their rapid walk. Miss Stanhope gently shook off Annis's hand, stepped to a counter, holding out her samples of zephyr, and addressing a clerk, remarked, "These are lovely colors!"

"Yes," said the girl, staring; "but what of it, ma'am?"

"My aunt wishes to match them," said Annis with dignity, resenting the half-insolent tone of the girl.

"Oh! Go to the next counter."

They moved on, Miss Stanhope smiling to herself at her own mistake, Annis with cheeks burning with indignation at the girl's rude stare and supercilious tone.

"Don't forget what you want this time, auntie," she whispered, as they paused before the next counter.

"No, dearie, but you mustn't mind your old auntie's blunders."

This time they were waited upon by a sweet-faced, modest maiden, who showed herself both obliging and respectful.

Miss Stanhope found just what she wanted. But Mildred was not ready to go yet, and while waiting for her, the old lady and the little girl amused themselves in examining the various contents of a showcase. Annis admired a necklace of amber beads, and Aunt Wealthy bought it for her, and another nearly like it for Fan.

"Anything else, ma'am?" asked the saleswoman as she wrapped them up.

"Yes, one of those little purses," said Miss Stanhope. "It is just what I want for small change and the trunk of my key, which I always carry in my pocket when travelling."

With a slight smile the saleswoman handed out several.

Miss Stanhope made her selection, and the query, "Anything else?" was repeated.

"Oh, yes!" exclaimed the old lady, as with sudden recollection. "Have you any remnants?"

"Remnants? Of what?"

"Dress goods."

"Oh, no. We keep nothing but trimmings and notions."

Mildred had finished her purchases, and coming up at that moment asked, "What is it, Aunt Wealthy?"

"Remnants."

"Oh, yes, of course you will want a supply of them," returned Mildred with a good-humored, slightly amused smile. "And yet what use can you make of them now? Even Annis has grown too large for a remnant to make her a dress."

"But there's Percy, and Zillah's boy, too," was the prompt reply. "Besides, they can be put to many uses about a house."

"Mightn't a remnant be big enough to make an apron for a lady even?" asked Annis.

"Yes," said Mildred, "and as I know auntie enjoys buying them, we will look for some."

They started at once on the quest, and Miss Stanhope was quite elated and triumphant on finding, in two different stores, two remnants of beautiful lawn, exactly alike, which together would make an ample dress pattern for Annis, besides others that could be utilized for aprons for her and Fan, dresses for the baby boys, or patchwork for quilts. Remnants were quite a hobby with the old lady, and she could never feel quite satisfied with the results of a shopping expedition that did not include some bargains in that line.

Returning to their hotel, they found letters from the Oaks and from home awaiting them.

"Ah, Milly," remarked the doctor with satisfaction as he glanced over his, "here are our measures. Rupert sends them."

"Then they are sure to be right," she responded.

"Measures for what?" inquired Miss Stanhope.

"Wallpaper and carpets for our new house. It is ready for them."

"Oh, how nice!" cried Annis, clapping her hands. "May I go with you to choose them, Brother Charlie?"

"We will be pleased to have your company and the benefit of your taste," was the gallant rejoinder, "Aunt Wealthy's also."

"Thank you," said Miss Stanhope absently. "I'm glad you're so near being done with your house, and I think it's a good plan to buy your papers here. But I'm afraid you'll have to put it in yourselves, for though I remember there were some painters in Pleasant Plains when I was there, I don't think there were any paperers at all, and everybody's walls were whitewashed, as far as I can recollect."

"But you know that was some years ago, auntie," said Mildred, "and a good many luxuries have been introduced since then, paperhangers among the rest."

"And the Keith family are so handy that they can easily do such work for themselves, if necessary," laughed Annis. "The boys really did paper our house, and paint it, too. Do you see, Milly," she said, holding up a letter, "this is from Elsie. She says she is having a lovely time all alone with her papa but misses us ever so much and hopes we will come back to spend next winter at the Oaks."

"Tell her, when you write, that we are greatly obliged, but the journey is quite too long to take twice a year," returned Mildred merrily.

"And we couldn't spend every winter away from father and mother," added Annis. "Oh, how glad I shall be to get home to them, and Fan, and the rest! How soon can we start?"

"Time's up in another week," answered the doctor, "and I judge, by the rate at which we've been going through the shopping and sightseeing, that we'll be ready by then."

CHAPTER FOURTH

Gold! gold! gold!
Bright and yellow, hard and cold!

— HOOD

A BEAUTIFUL SPRING day was drawing to a close as two persons — a young man and a maiden — seated themselves on a fallen tree on the western bank of the St. Joseph River. They had strolled a long distance from home, leaving the noise and bustle of the town far behind. They were a trifle weary with their walk, and it was pleasant to sit here and rest in the cool evening air, sweet with the scent of wildwood flowers, with the grass green about their feet and no sound to break the stillness save the song of the cricket, the gentle murmur of the breeze in the tree tops, and the soft ripple of the water flowing swiftly onward, so bright and clear that it reflected, as in a mirror, its own grassy wooded banks and the rich purple, gold, and amber of the sunset clouds, while the pebbly bottom, with fishes great and small darting here and there, could be distinctly seen.

For some time the two sat there silently, hand in hand, the girl's eyes gazing steadily down into the water, her companion's fixed upon her face with an expression of ardent admiration and intense, yearning affection. It was a noble countenance, at this moment thoughtful and grave, even to sadness.

"Ada, my love," he said at length, "it is a hard thing I am asking of you. I am ashamed of my selfishness."

"No, no! Do not talk so. How could I bear to let yo go alone, you who have no one in the wide world but me?" she answered in a low, tremulous tone, her eyes still upon the water. Then suddenly turning toward him, her face flushing with enthusiasm, her eyes shining through tears, she said, "But it is not you that ask if of me, Frank. No, not you, but One who has every right; for has He not redeemed me with His own precious blood? Is He not my Creator, Preserver, and bountiful Benefactor, and have I not given myself to Him, soul and body, in an everlasting covenant? And shall I keep back any part of the price? Oh, no, no! Let me but make sure that it is His voice I hear saying, 'This is the way; walk ye in it,' and I am ready to leave all and follow Him, though it be to the ends of the earth."

"My darling," he said with emotion, tightening his clasp of the hand he held, "you have the right spirit; you view this matter in the right light. Yes, we are His, both of us, and may our only question of duty ever be, 'Lord, what wilt thou have me to do?' But if we see it our duty to go, the sacrifice I make will be as nothing to yours, my sweet girl."

"Yet it will not be small, Frank. To leave forever one's dear native land is no slight thing,

especially when it is to live among heathen people—low, cruel, degraded idolators."

"That is true, and yet—oh, is there not joy in
the thought of telling the old, old story of Jesus
and His love to those who have never heard it,
and who, if we do not carry it to them, may never
hear it?"

"Yes, yes, indeed! And in the thought that we
are literally obeying His command, 'Go ye into all
the world and preach the Gospel to every creature.' And how very slight will be our suffering
and self-denial compared to His!"

"But, Frank, how shall we determine this question? How know whether we are truly called to
this great work? Ah, it does not seem possible that
I should ever be deemed worthy of such honor!"

"We will continue to make it a subject of constant, earnest prayer," he said, "asking to be
guided to a right decision. Also, we will open our
hearts to your parents and consult them. If they
refuse consent to your going, we will see in that
an indication that the Lord's will is not that we
should go. Laborers are needed here also, and it
may be that He will appoint us our work in this
part of His vineyard."

"Yes," she said, "I could never feel it right to go
if father and mother should oppose it. Yet I am
sure they will not, if they see reason to believe we
are called by the Master, for ever since I can
remember, their most ardent wish for their children has been that they might be entirely devoted
to His service."

At that moment the honored parents of whom
she spoke, sitting side by side in the vine-covered

porch of their home, resting after the labors of the day, were talking of their children and rejoicing in the well-founded belief that most, if not all, of them had already given themselves to that blessed service.

They spoke of Mildred and Annis, the eldest and youngest, now on the way home after their winter at the Oaks; of Rupert, their eldest son, a prosperous and highly respected man of business; Cyril, absent at college; Zillah, with her husband and babe, living just across the street; of Ada and her betrothed; and, lastly, of the only two just then in sight — Don and Fan — down in the garden, seated on a bench under a spreading tree, the lad whittling, his sister watching him, with hands lying idly in her lap.

There was languor in the droop of her slender figure. The eyes that rested now upon Don's face, now on his work, were unnaturally large and bright, and though a rich color glowed in her cheeks, her features were thin and sharp.

"Stuart," said Mrs. Keith, in low, slightly tremulous tones, gazing fixedly at Fan as she spoke, "I am growing uneasy about that child. She is not well. She scarcely complains but is losing flesh and strength very fast of late."

"Only because she is growing so rapidly, I think, Marcia," he said. "See what a brilliant color she has."

"Not the bloom of health, I fear," said the mother. "I am very glad Dr. Landreth will be here soon. I hope he may be able to do something for her."

"I hope so, indeed. Perhaps it is change of climate and scene she needs. Probably it would have been better had she gone with the others last fall."

"I don't know; it is too late to think of it now, but if Charlie recommends a trip, we must manage to give it to her."

"Certainly; and in that case you will have to go too, for I doubt if anything could induce Fan to leave her mother."

"No. What a dear, affectionate child she is! And how she and Don cling to each other."

In the pause that followed that last remark, Fan's low, clear tones came distinctly to their ears.

"Ah, now I see what you are making, Don. A spoon, isn't it?"

"Yes, it'll be very useful on the journey across the plains."

"Whose journey?"

"Mine," he said; then sang happily:

> *"O California! Oh, that's the land for me!*
> *I'm bound for Sacramento,*
> *With the washbowl on my knee."*

"That's the tune of *O Susannah*," she said as he ceased, "but where did you get those words?"

"Haven't you heard it before?" he asked. "They've been singing it all over town. The gold fever's raging, and a lot of fellows are talking of going off across the plains to the California diggings. If they do, I'd like to make one of the party."

The parents, who were silently listening, exchanged glances of mingled surprise and concern, while Fan exclaimed, "Oh, Don, you can't be in earnest?"

"You'd better believe I am," laughed the lad. "Why, it would be the greatest fun in the world, I think, to go and dig gold."

"Exceedingly hard work, my boy," Mr. Keith said, raising his voice that it might reach the lad.

Don started and turned his head. He had not thought of anyone but Fan hearing his talk.

"But we wouldn't mind working very hard indeed for a little while to make a fortune, father," he answered in a lively tone, springing up and advancing to the steps of the porch. Fan followed and seated herself upon them.

"Ah, but who can insure the making of the fortune?" asked Mr. Keith gravely. "Where one will succeed, Don, probably hundreds will fail and die of the great hardships to be encountered in the search for gold—the exhausting toil, scanty fare, and exposure to the inclemencies of the weather. It cannot fail to be a rough and toilsome life, full of danger and temptation, too, for the desperadoes and outlaws from all parts of the country, if not of the world, are always among the first to rush to such places. And even men who behaved respectably at home often throw off all restraint there and act like savages."

"Think, too, of the dangers to be encountered along the way, Don," said his mother. "A trackless wilderness to cross, supplies of food and water perhaps giving out, to say nothing of perils from wild beasts and hostile Indians."

"Oh, mother," he said, "if you'd ever been a boy, you'd know that danger has great attractions sometimes."

"But oh, Don," exclaimed Fan, "just think what

mother and I and all of us would be suffering from anxiety on your account!"

Ah, but you'd feel paid for it all when you saw me come home with my pockets full of gold!"

"Gold far too dearly bought, if you came back to us a rough, hardened man, instead of the dear boy you are now," said his mother.

"I've no notion of ever becoming a rough, mother mine," returned the lad in a half-playful tone. "And what is virtue worth that can't stand temptation?"

"Not much, my son," said his father gravely, "but what mockery to pray, 'Lead us not into temptation' and then rush needlessly into it. But let the subject drop, for I am quite resolved never to give my consent to so wild a project."

The boy's face clouded, but, accustomed to obedience, he ventured no reply. "Here, Fan, I'll give this to you," he said, handing her the now finished spoon.

"Thank you; it is very pretty," she returned, regarding it admiringly.

"Fan, dear, I think the dew is beginning to fall," said Mrs. Keith, rising. "Come in, come in both of you. We will adjourn to the sitting room."

They did so and were there presently joined by Frank and Ada, who came in hand in hand, their faces full of a strange mixture of joy and sorrow. Mrs. Keith sat in a low rocking chair, softly passing her hand over Fan's hair and cheek, the young girl having seated herself on a stool at her mother's side and laid her head in her lap.

They, as well as Mr. Keith and Don, seemed to be silently musing as the other two entered. But all four looked up at the sound of their footsteps, and Mrs. Keith, noticing the unusual expression of their countenances, asked a little anxiously, "What is it, Ada, my child?"

Ada opened her lips to reply, but no sound came from them. Hastily withdrawing her hand from Fran's, she sprang forward and knelt beside her sister.

"Mother, oh, mother, how can I ever leave you!" she exclaimed, tears coursing down her cheeks.

Mrs. Keith was much surprised, knowing of no adequate cause for such emotion, especially in one usually so calm and undemonstrative as Ada.

"Dear child," she said, caressing her, "we will hope never to be too far apart for frequent talks. Frank's present charge is but a few miles distant."

"But, mother, he thinks he is called to foreign missions," Ada returned in trembling tones. "Can you let me go? Can you give me to that work?"

The query, so sudden, so unexpected, sent a keen pang to the tender mother's heart. With a silent caress she drew her beloved child closer, and they mingled their tears together.

"What—what is this I hear, Frank?" asked Mr. Keith huskily, starting up and drawing nearer the little group, for Frank had followed Ada and stood looking down upon her, his features working with emotion.

With an effort he controlled it and in a few words gave the desired information. "He had for some time felt an increasing interest in the foreign work and in the desire to give himself to it should it be made plain that he was called of God to that part of the field."

"Oh, no, no!" cried Fan, putting her arms about her sister's neck, "we can't spare you. Why mayn't Frank work for the Master here as well as there? Laborers are needed in both places."

"Very true," said Frank, "and I trust our earnest desire is to be guided to that part of the vineyard where the Master would have us."

"It shall be my prayer that you may," said the mother with emotion, drawing Ada's head to a resting place on her breast as she spoke. "And dearly, dearly as I love my child, hard as it will be to part with her, I cannot hesitate for a moment if the Master calls her to go."

"No, nor can I," Mr. Keith said, sighing and bending down to stroke Ada's hair in tender, fatherly fashion.

CHAPTER FIFTH

Home is the resort
Of love, of joy, of peace, and plenty, where,
Supporting and supported, polish'd friends
And dear relations mingle into bliss.

—THOMSON'S *SEASONS*

THE SWEETEST OF May mornings. The sun shines brightly in a sky of heavenly blue, wherein float soft, fleecy clouds of snowy whiteness, casting faint shadows now here, now there, over the landscape. The forest trees have donned their spring robes of tender green, and at their feet the earth is carpeted with grass spangled with myriads of lovely wildflowers of varied hues. The air is redolent of their sweet breath and vocal with the songs of the birds in the treetops and all the pleasant sounds of rural life. Everything seems so bright, so fresh and new, that Annis, as the stage rolls rapidly onward, bringing her every moment nearer home, is almost wild with delight, while the older members of the party, if less demonstrative, are scarcely less happy.

They counted the miles as those at home were

counting the hours and the minutes. The journey from Philadelphia to Northern Indiana was far more tedious and wearisome in those days than it is now, and they were tired enough of travel to be glad to reach their journey's end. Rest would be delightful, but it was the thought of home and dear ones that constituted their chief joy.

The stage was due in Pleasant Plains just at noon, and today, having no hindrance from bad weather or bad roads, arrived punctually to the minute. The mail was dropped at the post office, a passenger at the hotel.

"To Lawyer Keith's next?" queried the driver, bending down from his high seat to bestow a roguish look and smile upon the impatient Annis.

"Yes," Dr. Landreth said, "we all belong there."

The stage was sweeping on again before he had half finished his sentence.

In another minute it drew up at the gate, and, oh, the greetings, the embraces that followed! The happy laughter, the looks of love, the tears of joy! For to the younger ones, the separation had seemed very long, as, indeed, so far as Miss Stanhope was concerned, it really had been.

The mutual affection of herself and niece was like that of mother and daughter, and they had not seen each other's faces for more than ten years. All the family loved the old lady, and she came in for her full share of the joyous welcome. Zillah was there with her husband and babe, and Ada had her betrothed by her side.

They sat down to dinner together, a large and happy party, most of them more disposed for conversation, however, than for doing justice to the fare upon which Celestia Ann had expended much thought and skill.

She was still with Mrs. Keith, devotedly attached to her and the whole family, and no one had bestowed a heartier hug upon Annis, Mildred, or even Aunt Wealthy than this somewhat forward but very warm-hearted maiden.

"You don't none o' ye eat half as much as you'd orter, considerin' what a sight o' trouble I took a-gettin' up this dinner," she grumbled as she waited on the table. "I remembered all your likings — Miss Milly's and Miss Stanhope's and Annis's — and done my best to foller 'em all. I broiled the chickings and smashed the 'taters and took a sight o' pains with the pies and puddin's, but you don't none o' you seem to 'preciate it, 'thout it's Don there, for here I'm a-carryin' out yer plates half full every time."

"That's because we have been so bountifully helped," said Mildred. "Father has heaped my plate with enough for two or three meals. So you mustn't feel hurt, Celestia Ann, for I assure you, I find your cookery delicious.

"So do I," said Annis. "I haven't tasted as good since we left the Oaks."

A chorus of complimentary remarks followed from the rest of the company, and Celestia Ann's wounded vanity was appeased.

"Fan," Dr. Landreth remarked, looking across the table at her, "I think you are the worst delinquent of all of us; you have eaten scarcely anything. And I suspect it is no new thing, for you have grown thin since I saw you last."

"Father says it's because I'm growing so fast,"

Fan said, blushing with embarrassment, as she felt that all eyes were turned upon her. "It's springtime, too, and that is apt to make one lose appetite and strength."

"I daresay you need change," remarked Annis wisely. "You see how well and strong I am. Don't you wish now you'd gone South with us?"

"No, I wouldn't have missed the nice time I've had with mother for anything," returned Fan, her eyes seeking her mother's face with a look of fond affection.

Mrs. Keith's answering smile was very sweet. "Yes," she said, "Fan and I have had a very pleasant, happy time together. And now, with all our dear ones restored," she said, glancing fondly from Annis to Mildred and Aunt Wealthy, "we shall be happier than ever."

"Home's a good place," remarked Don, pushing away his plate and settling himself back in his chair with the air of one whose appetite is fully satisfied. "But I, for one, would like to see something of the world."

"Time enough yet, my boy," remarked Dr. Landreth laughingly. "You may well feel thankful that you are not forced out into it now, before you are fully prepared for the battle of life."

Don looked slightly vexed and impatient. "Yes," he said, "that's the way you all talk. It's wait, wait, wait, instead of 'strike while the iron's hot.'"

"What iron?" inquired Mildred, with a look half of interest, half of amusement.

"I want to go to California and dig gold," blurted out the boy, "but father and mother won't hear of it, though there's a large party starting from here next week."

"Oh, Don, what an idea!" exclaimed Mildred. "I'm glad you can't win consent."

"I too," said the doctor. "Don, if you knew what the life is, you would not want to try it. I have had experience of it, you remember."

"Who are going from here?" asked Mildred.

Quite a list of names was given in reply, including those of several of her familiar acquaintance.

"How will they go?" she asked, a look of grave concern coming over her face.

"Across the plains," answered Rupert, "in wagons drawn by ox teams. It can't fail to be a slow and toilsome journey."

"And a dangerous one as well," added his mother with a deprecating look at Don.

"Yes, I know," said the lad, "but I'm fairly spoiling for a taste of that, mother," he added with a laugh.

She shook her head. "Ah, my boy, I wish you knew when you were well off."

They left the table and flocked into the parlor, but Mrs. Keith drew Dr. Landreth aside and whispered in his sympathizing ear her anxiety in regard to Fan. She described every symptom without reserve, then asked, with a look of deep solicitude, "What do you think of the case?"

"You must allow me a little time to study it, mother," he said, "but I trust it will prove nothing serious. She must have rest, a tonic, a daily walk of such length as she can take without undue fatigue, and frequent drives. Those I can give her as I visit my country patients."

"Thank you," she said. "I have been very impatient for your return on the dear child's account."

"What is that you are talking of, mother?" Mildred asked, joining them.

"Of Fan, Milly. She hasn't seemed well for some time, and I have been consulting the doctor about her."

Mildred's eyes filled. "My darling little sister!" she exclaimed. "I hope it is nothing serious?" She turned an eager, inquiring look upon her husband.

"We will hope not, Milly," he said cheerfully. "As your father says, she is growing fast, and besides, this warm spring weather is apt to cause a feeling of languor. I trust that with tender care and watchfulness we may be able to help her to grow into strong, healthful womanhood."

Both mother and sister looked relieved, and presently they rejoined the others.

Frank Osborne was just taking leave. He must return to the duties of his charge and might not see them again for several days.

Ada left the room with her betrothed for a few last words.

When she entered the parlor again, Aunt Wealthy, making room for her on the sofa by her side, asked, "Are you to be settled near Pleasant Plains, dear? I hope so, for it would be very hard for you to go far from father and mother, brothers and sisters, and for them to have you do so."

Ada could not answer for a moment, and when she found her voice, it was tremulous with emotion.

"We do not know yet, Aunt Wealthy," she said. "It will be hard to leave home and dear ones, but we are ready and willing to go wherever the Lord may send us."

"Ada, what do you mean?" asked Mildred. "Surely, Frank has no thought of seeking a foreign field?"

"Can't you give me up if the Master calls me away, Milly?" asked Ada, taking her sister's hand and pressing it fondly in hers.

"In that case, I would not dare hold you back if I could. His claim is far stronger than mine," Mildred said with emotion.

Then the whole story came out, and the matter was discussed in a family council.

But they could go no farther than the expression of their opinions and wishes. Frank had already offered himself to the Board of Foreign Missions, and his going depended upon their acceptance or rejection.

"I hope they'll say, 'No, we think you can find enough to do where you are,'" said Annis playfully but with eyes full of tears, putting her arms around Ada's neck and laying her cheek to hers as she spoke. "I'm sure I don't know what we should ever do without you!" she went on. "I don't like to have you go away even as far as the country church where Frank preaches now."

"Well, dear, we won't borrow trouble. 'Sufficient unto the day is the evil thereof,'" Ada said, holding her close and fondly kissing the rosy cheek.

"'And as thy days, so shall thy strength be,'" added Mrs. Keith. "Our blessed Master will never lay upon any of us a heavier burden than He gives us strength to bear."

"No," said Rupert. "And now—to turn to a pleasanter theme than the possibility of losing Ada—Mildred, don't you want to go and take a look at your new house, you, and the doctor, and anybody else that cares to see it?"

"Oh, is it done?" cried Annis, suddenly forgetting her grief and loosening her hold of Ada to clap her hands with delight.

"Yes, all but the papering and painting," replied Rupert.

"I move we all go in a body," said Mildred merrily.

"So many of us! People would stare," objected Fan with her usual timidity.

"What matter if they should?" laughed Mildred. "But it is only a step, and there are very few neighbors near enough to watch our proceedings."

"And why shouldn't we be independent and do as we please?" remarked Don loftily. "I vote in the affirmative. Come, let's go."

"A dozen of us, without counting the babies," murmured Fan with a little sigh. But she tried on the dainty white muslin sunbonnet her mother handed her, took Don's offered arm, and went with the rest.

As they passed from room to room, Mildred's eyes shone with pleasure.

The plan of the house was the joint work of herself and husband, embodying their ideas in regard to comfort and convenience. Rupert had been left in charge of the work during their absence and had acquitted himself of the trust to their entire satisfaction.

Both returned him warm thanks, Mildred saying again and again, "I am delighted, Ru. You have not forgotten or neglected the least of our wishes."

"I am very glad it pleases you, Milly," he said with a gratified look. "It has been a labor of love to attend to it for you."

"It is quite done except the work of the paperers and painters, is it not?" queried Aunt Wealthy.

"Yes," said the doctor, "and we will set the painters at work tomorrow, the paperers as soon as our boxes of goods arrive."

CHAPTER SIXTH

We all do fade as a leaf.

—ISAIAH 64:6

DR. LANDRETH AND Mildred gladly availed themselves of a pressing invitation to take up their old quarters at her father's until such time as their own house should be entirely ready for occupancy.

There was general rejoicing among the family that that time was not yet, for they were so glad to have Mildred with them once more. Nor did she regret the necessity for continuing a little longer a member of her father's household, especially considering that this was Ada's last summer at home.

There was always a community of interests among them, a sharing of each other's burdens. Thus, all were very busy, now helping Mildred prepare bedding and napery, curtains, etc., and now helping Ada with her trousseau and everything that could be thought of to add to her comfort in the foreign land to which she was going, for in due time Frank Osborne received word that he had been accepted by the Board.

Many tears were shed over that news, yet not

one of those who loved her so dearly would have held Ada back from the service to which the Master had called her. She was His far more than theirs, and they were His and would gladly give to Him of their best and dearest.

Others had given up their loved ones to go in search of gold—the wealth of this world that perishes with the using—parting from them with almost breaking hearts. And should they shrink from a like sacrifice for Him who had bought them with His own precious blood, to send the glad news of His salvation to those perishing for lack of knowledge?

The train of emigrants for California had left at the set time, their relatives and friends—in some cases wives and children—parting from them as from those who were going almost out of the world and might never be seen again.

A journey to California is accounted no great thing in these days, when one may travel all the way by rail, but in those times, when it was by ox teams and wagons across thousands of miles of trackless wilderness over which wild beasts and hostile Indians ranged, it was a perilous undertaking.

So they who went and they who stayed behind parted as those who had but slight hope of ever meeting again in this lower world.

Nearly the whole town gathered to see the train of wagons set forth, and even Don Keith, as he witnessed the final leave-takings, the clinging embraces, the tearful, sobbing adieus, was not more than half sorry that he was not going along.

Fan drew the acknowledgment from him later

in the day, when she overhead him softly singing to himself:

> *"'I jumped aboard the old ox team,*
> *and cracked my whip so free;*
> *And every time I thought of home,*
> *I wished it wasn't me.'"*

"Yes, that would have been the way with you, Don, I'm sure," Fan said. "So be wise in time, and don't try it, even if father should consent."

"I don't know," he said, turning toward her with a roguish twinkle in his eye; "I think another part of the song suits me better:

> *"'We'll dig the mountains down,*
> *We'll drain the rivers dry;*
> *A million of the rocks bring home,*
> *So, ladies, don't you cry.'"*

"That's easier said than done, Don," Fan remarked with a grave, half-sad look. "Oh, brother dear, don't let the love of gold get possession of you!"

"I don't love it for itself, Fan—I hope I never shall—but for what it can do, what it can buy."

"It cannot buy the best things," she said, looking at him with dewy eyes. "It cannot buy heaven, it cannot buy love, or health, or freedom from pain, no, nor a clear conscience or quiet mind. It will seem of small account when one comes to die."

"Don't talk of dying," he said a little uneasily. "We needn't think much about that yet—you and I, who are both so young."

"But a great many die young, Don, even younger than we are today."

She laid her hand upon his arm as she spoke and looked into his eyes with tender sadness.

As he noted the words, the look, and the extreme attenuation of the little hand, a sharp pang shot through his heart. Could it be that Fan, his darling sister, was going to die? The thought had never struck him before. He knew that she was not strong, that the doctor was prescribing for her and taking her out driving every day., and he had perceived that the older members of the family, particularly his mother, were troubled about her, but had thought it was only permanent loss of health they feared.

But the idea of death was too painful to be encouraged, and he put it hastily from him. How could he ever do without Fan? There was less than two years between them, and they had always been inseparable. No, he would not allow himself to think of the possibility that she was about to pass away from him to "that bourne whence no traveller returns."

He was glad that Annis joined them at that moment in mirthful mood.

"What's so funny, Ann? he asked, seeing a merry twinkle in her eye.

"Oh, just some of Aunt Wealthy's odd mistakes. She was talking about that first winter we spent here, when she was with us, you remember. She said, 'The weather was very cold. Many's the time I've had hard work to get my hands up, my hair was so cold.' Then she was telling something her doctor in Lansdale told her about a very dirty family he was called to see. A child had the croup, and he made them put it into a hot bath. He was still there the next morning and saw them getting breakfast, and telling about it, Aunt Wealthy said, 'They used the water to make the coffee that the child was bathed in.'"

"The doctor stayed and took breakfast with them, I suppose?" said Don dryly.

"Not he," laughed Annis; "he said he was very hungry, and they were kindly urgent with him to stay and eat, but he preferred taking a long, cold ride before breaking his fast."

"I admire his self-denial," remarked Don with gravity. "Anything else of interest from Aunt Wealthy?"

"Yes," said Annis, "she was speaking of some religious book she had been reading, and she said she had bought it from a portcollier. And yesterday, when I complained that I hated to darn my stockings, she said, 'Oh, my dear, always attend to that. A stocking in a hole, or indeed a glove either, is a sure sign of a sloven.'"

"Then," said Don gravely, "I trust you will be careful never to drop yours into holes."

"Don't let us make game of dear, kind old Aunt Wealthy," Fan said in a gentle, deprecating tone.

"Oh, no, not for the world!" cried Annis, "but one can't help laughing at her funny mistakes. And indeed, she is as ready to do so as anyone else."

"Yes, and it's very nice in her," said Don.

For a while after that, Don watched Fan closely, but noticing that she was always cheerful, bright, and interested in all that was going on, he dismissed his fears with the consoling idea that there could not be anything serious amiss with her.

By midsummer Mildred was fairly settled in her own house, and work for Ada was being pushed forward with energy and dispatch.

The wedding—a very quiet affair—took place in September. A few days later the youthful pair bade a long farewell to relatives and friends and started for New York, whence they were to sail, early in October, for China.

The parting was a sore trial to all, and no one seemed to feel it more than Fan.

"Ada! Ada!" she sobbed, clinging about her sister's neck, "I shall never, never see you again in this world!"

"Don't say that, darling," responded Ada in tones tremulous with emotion. "I am not going out of the world, and probably we may be back again in a few years on a visit."

"But I shall not be here," murmured Fan. "Something tells me I am going on a longer journey than yours."

"I hope not," Ada said, scarcely able to speak. "You are depressed now because you are not well, but I trust you will soon grow strong again and live many years to be a comfort and help to father and mother. I used to plan to be the one to stay at home and take care of them in their old age, but now, I think, that is to be your sweet task."

"I'd love to do it," Fan said. "I'd rather do that than anything else, if it should please God to make me well and strong again."

"And if not, dear," Ada said, drawing her into a closer embrace, "He will give you strength for whatever He has in store for you, whether it be a life of invalidism or an early call to that blessed land where 'the inhabitants shall not say, I am sick.'"

"Yes," was the whispered response, "and sometimes I feel that it is very sweet just to leave it all with Him and have no choice of my own."

"Thank God for that, my darling little sister!" Ada exclaimed with emotion. "I have no fear for you now, for I am sure you are ready to go if it shall please the Master to call you to Himself."

This little talk took place early in the day of Ada's departure, she having stolen into Fan's room as soon as she was dressed to ask how the invalid had passed the night.

They were interrupted by the mother's entrance on the same errand.

Embracing both as they stood together, she said, "My two dear daughters." Then to Fan: "You are up and dressed early for an ailing one, my child."

"Yes, mother, I couldn't lie in bed this morning, the last that we shall have Ada with us," Fan answered with a sob, holding her sister in a tighter clasp.

"The last for a time," Mrs. Keith returned cheerfully, though the tears trembled in her eyes. "Missionaries come home sometimes on a visit, you know, and we will look forward to that."

"And besides that, we know that we shall meet in the Father's house on high, meet never to part again," whispered Ada, pressing her lips to her mother's cheek, then to Fan's.

"But to be forever with the Lord," added Mrs.

Keith. "Now, Fan dear, sit down in your easy chair till the call to breakfast, and after this try to follow your Brother Charlie's advice — taking a good rest in the morning, even if you have to breakfast in bed."

Unconsciously to herself as well as to others, the excitement of the preparations for Ada's wedding and life in a foreign land had been giving Fan a fictitious strength, which immediately on her sister's departure deserted her and left her prostrate upon her bed.

Mother and the remaining sisters nursed her with the tenderest care, and after a time she rallied so far as to be about the house again and drive out occasionally in pleasant weather. But the improvement was only temporary, and before the winter was over it became apparent to all that Fan was passing away to the better land.

To all but Don and Annis. He refused to believe it, and she, with the hopefulness of childhood, was always "sure dear darling Fan would soon be better."

For many weeks the mother shrank from having her fears confirmed. Often, as she noted the gravity and sadness of the doctor's face, the question trembled upon her tongue, but she could not bring herself to speak it. But one day, seeing, as she thought, a deeper shade of anxiety upon his face than ever before, she followed him from the room.

"Charlie," she said in faltering accents, "I must know the truth though my heart break. Tell me, must my child die?"

"Dear mother," he said, taking her hand in his

and speaking with strong emotion, "I wish I could give you hope, but there is none. She may linger a month or two but not longer."

"Oh, how shall I ever tell her!" sobbed the mother. "Her, my timid little Fan, who has always been afraid to venture among strangers, always clung so tenaciously to home and mother!"

"I think she knows it," he said, deeply moved. "I have seen it again and again in the look she has given me. And I doubt not that God is fulfilling to her the promise, 'As thy days, so shall thy strength be.'"

"May the Lord forgive my unbelief!" she said. "I know that He is ever faithful to His promises."

Returning to the sick room, she found Fan lying with closed eyes, a very sweet and peaceful expression on her face.

Bending over her, she kissed the sweet lips, and a hot tear fell on the child's cheek.

Her blue eyes opened wide, and her arm crept round her mother's neck.

"Dearest mother, don't cry," she whispered. "I am glad to go and be with Jesus. You know it says, 'He shall gather the lambs with His arm and carry them in His bosom.' I shall never be afraid or timid lying there. Oh, He will love me and take care of me, and someday bring you there, too, and father, and all my dear ones. And oh, how happy we shall be!"

"Yes, love," the mother said, "yours is a blessed lot—to be taken so soon from the sins and sorrows of earth. 'Thine eyes shall see the King in His beauty: they shall behold the land that is very far off. . . . Thine eyes shall see Jerusalem a quiet habitation, a tabernacle that shall not be taken down; not one of the stakes thereof shall ever be removed, neither shall any of the cords thereof be broken. But there the glorious Lord will be unto us a place of broad rivers and streams. . . . And the inhabitant shall not say, I am sick: the people that dwell therein shall be forgiven their iniquity.'"

"Such sweet words," said Fan. "Oh, I am glad Ada has gone to tell the poor heathen of this dear Saviour! How could I bear to die if I did not know of Him and His precious blood that cleanseth from all sin!"

"Dearest child, do you feel quite willing to go?" Mrs. Keith asked, softly stroking her hair and gazing upon her with tear-dimmed eyes.

"Yes, mother, I do now, though at first it seemed very sad, very hard to leave you all to go and lie down all alone in the dark grave. But I don't think of that now; I think of being with Christ in glory, near Him and like Him. Oh, mother, how happy I shall be!"

The door opened, and Mildred came softly in. She bent over Fan, her eyes full of tears, her features working with emotion. She had just learned from her husband what he had told her mother.

"Dear Milly," Fan said, putting an arm about her neck, her lips to her cheek, "has Brother Charlie told you?"

Mildred nodded, unable to speak.

"Don't fret," Fan said tenderly. "I am not sorry, though I was at first. What is dying but going home? Oh, don't you remember how John tells us in the Revelation about the great multitude that stood before the throne and before the Lamb clothed in white robes and with palms in their hands? And how the angel told him, 'There are they which came out of great tribulation, and have washed their robes, and made them white in the blood of the Lamb. Therefore are they before the throne of God, and serve Him day and night in His temple; and He that sitteth on the throne shall dwell among them.'?

"'They shall hunger no more, neither thirst anymore; neither shall the sunlight on them, nor any heat. For the Lamb which is in the midst of the throne shall feed them, and shall lead them unto living fountains of waters: and God shall wipe away all tears from their eyes.'

"Mother," she said, turning to her with a glad, eager look, "may I not hope to be one of them if I trust in Jesus and bear with patience and resignation whatever He sends?"

"Surely, my darling," Mrs. Keith answered in tremulous tones. "They stand in the righteousness of Christ, and so will all who truly come to Him and trust only in His atoning sacrifice."

"Dear, dear Fan," whispered Mildred, caressing her with fast-falling tears, "I don't know how to give you up. And oh, darling—but I wish I had been a better sister to you!"

"Why, Milly, how could you have been?" Fan said with a look and tone of great surprise. "I am sure you were always the best and kindest of sisters to me."

"No, not always," Mildred said sorrowfully. "I used to be very impatient with you at times when you were a little thing given to mischief. But I feel now that I would give worlds never to have spoken a cross word to you."

"Ah, we must often have made a great deal of trouble with our mischievous pranks—Cyril, Don, and I"—Fan said with a slight smile. "Don't reproach yourself for scolding us, Milly. I am sure we deserved it all, and more."

Mr. Keith was told the doctor's opinion that day, but the rest of the family were left in ignorance of it for the present.

It was from Fan herself that Don learned it at length. They were alone together, and he was talking hopefully of the time when she would be up and about again, and he would take her boating in the river, riding or driving, and they would enjoy, as of old, long rambles through the woods in search of the sweet wildflowers that would come again with the warm spring days.

"Dear Don, dear, dear brother!" she said, giving him a look of yearning affection, "do you not know that when those days come I shall be walking the streets of the New Jerusalem, gathering such fruits and flowers as earth cannot yield?"

A sudden paleness overspread his face, his eyes filled, and his lip quivered. "Fan! Fan!" he cried with a burst of emotion, "it can't be so! You are too young to die, and we can't spare you. You are weak and low-spirited now, but you will feel better when the bright spring days come."

She smiled sweetly, pityingly upon him, softly stroking his hair with her thin white hand as he bent over her.

"No, dear Don, I am not low-spirited," she said. "I am full of joy in the prospect of being so soon with my Saviour. Brother Charlie says it will not be very long now; a week or two, perhaps."

"I can't believe it! I won't believe it!" he groaned. "While there's life, there's hope. It can't be that you *want* to go away and leave me, Fan?" he said, and his tone was gently, lovingly reproachful.

"No," she said, her voice trembling, "it is pain to think of parting from you and the rest, especially our dear, dear mother, and yet I am glad to go to be with Jesus. Oh, how I long to see His face, to bow at His feet, and thank Him 'for the great love wherewith He hath loved us.'"

"But you have a great deal to live for. We all love you so."

"'In thy presence is fullness of joy,'" she repeated; "'at thy right hand there are pleasures forever more.'

"'For we know that if our earthly house of this tabernacle were dissolved, we have a building of God, an house not made with hands, eternal in the heavens.'

"'Henceforth there is laid up for me a crown of righteousness, which the Lord, the righteous Judge, shall give me at that day: and not to me only, but unto all them also that love His appearing.'

"'For since the beginning of the world men have not heard, nor perceived by the ear, neither hath the eye seen, O God, beside thee, what He hath prepared for him that waiteth for Him.' Oh, Don, would you keep me from it all?"

"Just for a while," he said, struggling for composure. "It is too dreadful to have you die so young."

"'Blessed are the dead who die in the Lord from henceforth,'" she repeated. "'My people shall dwell in a peaceable jabotatom, and in sure dwellings, and in quiet resting places.' Oh, Don, think of the golden streets of the New Jerusalem, the beautiful river of the water of life, the tree of life with its twelve manner of fruits, the white robes, the golden harps, the crowns of glory; and that there will be no more sickness, or sorrow, or pain; no more sin, no night, no need of a candle to light them, nor of the sun, or the moon, the glory of God and Christ lighting it always.

"Think of Jesus making me to lie down in green pastures and leading me beside still waters."

"You seem just as sure, Fan, as if you were already there," he said in admiring wonder.

"Yes, Don, because the promise is sure — the promise of Jesus, 'I give unto them eternal life, and they shall never perish; neither shall any pluck them out of my hand.'"

Celestia Ann came in at that moment, carrying a china cup and plate on a small waiter covered with a snowy napkin.

"Here, I've fetched you a bit o' cream toast and a cup o' tea, Fan," she said. "I hope you kin eat it. But, dear me, you're lookin' all tuckered out. I'll bet Don's been a-makin' you talk a heap more'n was good fer ye. Now we jest clear out, Don, and let's see if I can't be a better nurse."

"I didn't mean to hurt her," Don said gruffly, trying to hide the pain in his heart.

"No, and you haven't," said Fan, gazing lovingly after him as he turned to go. "If I've talked too much, it was my own doing."

Don, hurrying downstairs and into the parlor, which he expected to find empty, came suddenly into the midst of a little group—his father, mother, and Mildred—conversing together in subdued tones.

He was beating a hasty retreat, thinking he had intruded upon a private interview, when his father called him back.

"We have nothing to conceal from you, Don," he said in tremulous tones, and the lad, catching sight of the faces of his mother and sister, perceived that they had both been weeping. "I suppose you know that—" Mr. Keith paused, unable to proceed.

"Is it about Fan?" Don asked huskily. "Yes, sir, she has just told me. But oh, I can't believe it! We must do something to save her!" he burst out in a paroxysm of grief.

"What's the matter?" cried Annis, coming dancing into the room in her usual light-hearted fashion but startled into soberness at the sight of Don's emotion and the grief-stricken countenances of the others.

Her mother motioned her to her side, and putting an arm about her, kissed her tenderly, the tears streaming over her face. "Annis, dear," she said, in broken accents, "perhaps we ought not to grieve. Fan is so happy, but it makes our hearts sad to know that very soon we shall see her beloved face no more upon earth."

"Mother!" cried Annis, hiding her face on her mother's breast and bursting into wild weeping, "Oh, mother, mother, it can't be that she's going to die! She can never bear to go away from you!"

"Yes, dear, she can," was the weeping reply. "She finds Jesus nearer and dearer than her mother, and how can I thank Him enough that it is so?"

"We have sent for Cyril," Mr. Keith said, addressing Don and handing him a letter. "He hopes to be with us tomorrow. She could not go without seeing him once more."

A little later Don, left alone with Mildred, asked, "Oh, Milly, is there no hope, no possibility of a favorable change?"

"None so far as man can see," she answered through her tears and sobs. "But with God all things are possible."

"I've been talking with her," he said presently, when he could control his emotion sufficiently to speak. "She told me herself that—that she was—going away. And she seemed so happy, so utterly without fear, that I could hardly believe it was our timid little Fan—always shrinking so from going among strangers."

"Yes," said Mildred, "what a triumph of faith! Her fearlessness is not from any lack of a deep sense of sin but because she is trusting in the imputed righteousness of Christ. She trusts Him fully, and so her peace is like a river. It continually brings to my mind that sweet text in Isaiah, 'And the work of righteousness shall be peace; and the effect of righteousness quietness and assurance forever.'"

And so it was to the very end. The sweet young Christian passed away so calmly and peacefully that her loved ones watching beside her bed scarce could tell the precise moment when her spirit took its flight.

There was no gloom in the deathbed scene, and there seemed little about the grave as they laid her body tenderly down there to rest till the resurrection morn, knowing that the spirit was even then rejoicing in the presence and love of her Redeemer.

CHAPTER SEVENTH

Heaven, the perfection of all that can
Be said, or thought, riches, delight, or harmony,
Health, beauty: and all these not subject to
The waste of time, but in their height eternal.

—SHIRLEY

"WE HAVE NO need to weep for her, my darling," Mr. Dinsmore said, softly stroking Elsie's hair as she lay sobbing in his arms, an open letter in her hand.

"No, papa, not for her, I know, but for the others. See, Annis's letter is all blistered with her tears, and she says it seems at times as if her heart would break. And Don—oh, she says Don is almost wild with grief, that he tells her he can hardly bear to be in the house, it is so lonely and desolate without Fan."

"Yes, I have no doubt they miss her sorely, yet time will assuage their grief. They will come to think less of their own loss and more of her blessedness."

Elsie lifted her face and wiped away her tears. "Is it not wonderful, papa," she said, "that Fan, always so timid and retiring, always clinging so to her mother and home, should be so willing and even glad to go?"

"Yes," he said, "it shows what the grace of God can do. She must have been given a very strong sense of her Saviour's love and presence with her as she passed through the valley of the shadow of death. It helps one to stronger faith in the precious promise, 'As thy days, so shall thy strength be.'"

Rose, sitting by reading a letter with fast-falling tears, wiped them away at that and, looking up, said, "Let me read you some things that Mildred tells me about her last hours."

"We will be glad to hear them," Mr. Dinsmore answered, and she began:

"'It was the loveliest deathbed scene—no fear, no desire to stay. As I stood beside her, an hour or two before the messenger came, I leaned over her and repeated the words, "The eternal God is thy refuge, and underneath are the everlasting arms."

"'She looked up with the sweetest smile. "Yes," she said, "Jesus is with me, and I am not afraid; He will carry me safely through the river."

"'Mother added: "And to a beautiful home— one of many mansions He has prepared for His people. You may be sure it is very lovely, very delightful, with everything you can possibly desire; for the wealth of the universe is His. He has all power in heaven and in earth, and you, for whom He has been making it ready, are dearer far to His heart than to mine.

"'"Eye hath not seen, nor ear heard, neither have entered into the heart of man, the things that God hath prepared for them that love Him."

"'Her look was ecstatic as she listened. "Oh,

how happy I shall be!" she exclaimed. "And it will seem only a very little while till you will all join me there."

"'She has brought heaven very near to us all,' Mildred added. 'It seems far more real to me than it ever did before. She has entered into the joy of the Lord, and we cannot mourn at all for her, though our hearts are sore with our own loss.

"'"Precious in the sight of the Lord is the death of His saints." Does He not gather them home with joy and rejoicing to the mansions His love has made beautiful beyond compare for them? I think our little Fan was so dear to Him that He could no longer spare her to us, nor was He willing to leave her any longer in this world of sin and suffering. That is our mother's feeling, father's, too, I think; and no one could be more resigned, more perfectly submissive, than they are.'"

"Yes, Marcia is a devoted Christian," Mr. Dinsmore said. Drawing Elsie into a closer embrace, he added, "I feel deeply for her in this sore bereavement."

He was asking himself, as again and again he pressed his lips to his daughter's fair brow, how he could ever endure such a loss.

There had been a steady correspondence between Rose and Mildred, Annis and Elsie, ever since the winter spent at the Oaks by Dr. and Mrs. Landreth and Annis.

Housekeeping cares and discussions in regard to the best manner of rearing their little ones filled no small part of the letters of the two young mothers.

Elsie and Annis wrote of their studies and

amusements and of the everyday occurrences in each family.

Thus Annis had learned about the life Elsie and her father led together while Rose was absent, of their journey to Philadelphia when he found himself able to go for his wife and little Horace, the visit there, and the return trip. Elsie had been kept informed, among other events, of the progress of Fan's sickness, and the letter received today had given an account of her death and burial.

"Papa?" Elsie asked, lifting her weeping eyes to his face, "What can I say to comfort poor Annis?"

"Just what I have been asking myself in regard to Marcia," he remarked with a deep-drawn sigh.

"And I about Mildred," Rose said, echoing the sigh. "I know of scarcely anything that is more delicate and difficult than the writing of a letter of condolence."

"It is extremely so in a case where there is any doubt of the happiness of the departed," Mr. Dinsmore said, "but comparatively easy when we know that to the dear one gone to be absent from the body is to be present with the Lord. Also that the mourners are of those who have a good hope through grace that it shall be so with themselves."

"I shall look for Bible words," Elsie said, leaving her father's knee to get her own little copy lying on a table near at hand.

"Bring it here, and let us look it over together," her father said, and obeying with alacrity, she again seated herself upon his knee.

Rose brought another Bible and a concordance and joined them in their search for whatever the blessed Book could tell them of the employments and enjoyments of heaven. They found it spoken of as a rest, as the Father's house, a heavenly country, the kingdom of Christ and of God, that they who overcome and reach that glorious place shall eat of the hidden manna, shall walk with Christ in white; that He will wipe away all tears from their eyes; that He will feed them and lead them unto living fountains of waters; that He will dwell among them; and they shall serve Him day and night in His temple.

That "they shall hunger no more, neither thirst any more; neither shall the sun light on them, nor any heat"; that they have palms of victory, white robes, and crowns and harps of gold; and that they stand before the throne and sing a new song, which no man can learn but those who are redeemed from the earth.

"And God shall wipe away all tears from their eyes; and there shall be no more death, neither sorrow, nor crying, neither shall there be any more pain: for the former things are passed away."

"Papa," said Elsie, "Enna told me once she didn't want to go to heaven and stand and sing all the time; she would get tired of that. I feel as if I should never grow weary of singing God's praise. I love those words of one of our hymns:

> *"When we've been there*
> *Ten thousand years,*
> *Bright shining as the sun,*
> *We've no less days*
> *To sing God's praise*
> *Than when we first begun.'*

"But surely singing is not the only employment there; for here in the twenty-first chapter of Revelation it says, 'And the nations of them which are saved shall walk in the light of it.' Then in the third verse of the next chapter, 'The throne of God and the Lamb shall be in it; and His servants shall serve Him.' Don't you think that means that He will give us some work to do for Him?"

Her face was full of an eager joy.

"Yes," Mr. Dinsmore said, "I do. Just what it will be the Bible does not tell us, but to those who love the Master, it must be a delight to do whatever He bids. The rest of heaven will not be that of inaction but the far more enjoyable one of useful employment without any sense of weariness.

"Perhaps He may sometimes send His redeemed ones on errands of mercy or consolation to the inhabitants of this or some other world."

"How sweet that would be!" exclaimed Elsie joyously. "Papa, if I should go first, what happiness it would be to come back sometimes and comfort you in your hours of sadness."

"I should rather have you here in the body," he said, tightening his clasp about her waist.

"God has not seen fit to gratify idle curiosity in regard to these matters," he resumed, "but He has told us enough to leave no room for doubt that heaven is an abode of transcendent bliss."

"Yes, papa, just to know that we will be forever with the Lord—near Him and like Him—is enough to make one long to be there. Dear Fan! How blest she is! Who could wish her back again?"

"No one who loves her with an unselfish love. And now I think we may write our letters."

"No doubt they already know all that we can tell them, for they are students of the Word, every one," observed Rose. "Yet it does one good to have these precious truths repeated many times."

"Yes," said her husband, "we are so prone to forgetfulness and unbelief, and Satan is so constantly on the watch to snatch away the word out of our hearts and destroy our comfort, if he could do nothing more."

"Papa," said Elsie, "I sometimes feel so afraid of him, then I remember that Jesus is so much stronger, and I seem to run right into His arms and am full of joy that there I am so safe. You know He says of His people, 'I give unto them eternal life; and they shall never perish, neither shall any pluck them out of my hand.'"

"No, not all the powers of hell can do it, for 'He is able to save them to the uttermost that come unto God by Him.' He said, 'All power is given unto me in heaven and in earth.' And 'I am persuaded that neither death, nor life, nor angels, nor principalities, nor powers, nor things present, nor things to come, nor height, nor depth, nor any other creature, shall be able to separate us from the love of God, which is in Christ Jesus our Lord.'"

CHAPTER EIGHTH

Farewell; God knows when we shall meet again.

MILDRED WAS IN her pretty sitting room busily plying her needle, little Percy playing about the floor—rolling a ball here and there.

Both mother and child were neatly attired—the little one in spotless white, his golden curls hanging about his neck and half shading a round rosy face with big blue eyes; the mother in a dark cashmere, which fell in soft folds around her graceful figure and was relieved at throat and wrists by dainty white ruffles of lace. Her hair was becomingly arranged, and she had never presented a more attractive appearance, even in the days of her girlhood.

Mildred was not one of those who are less careful to please the husband than the lover. She studied Charlie's tastes and wishes even more carefully now than had been her wont before they were married. Perhaps in that lay the secret of his undiminished and lover-like devotion to her.

Both he and she had a great aversion to mourning; therefore, they were glad that Fan had particularly requested that none should be worn for her.

It was a little past their usual hour for tea, and the open dining room door gave a glimpse of a table covered with snowy damask and glittering with polished silver, cut glass, and china. But Dr. Landreth was closeted with someone in his office on the other side of the hall, and his wife waited the departure of the patient a trifle anxiously, fearing that her carefully prepared viands would lose their finest flavor, if not be rendered quite tasteless by standing so long.

"Shall I make de waffles in de iron, ma'am?" asked Gretchen, coming to the door.

"No, not yet," said Mildred, "they would be cooked too soon. The doctor likes them best just as they are ready."

"De iron gets too hot," observed the girl.

"Yes, take it off, Gretchen. I can't tell just how soon the doctor will be in, so we will have to keep him waiting while we heat the iron."

The girl went back to her kitchen, and Percy, dropping his toys, came to his mother's side with a petition to be taken into her lap.

She laid aside her sewing, took him on her knee, and amused him with stories suited to his baby mind.

At length she heard the office door open, and a familiar voice saying, "Well, Charlie, I shall take the matter into consideration. Am much obliged for your advice, whether I follow it or not."

Mildred hastily set Percy down and ran to the door.

"Rupert," she said, "won't you stay to tea?"

"Thank you, Milly, not tonight," he answered. "I have already declined a warm invitation from Charlie." And with a hasty "Goodbye," he hurried away.

Mildred thought her husband's face unusually grave, even troubled, as he came into the sitting room, and a sudden fear assailed her.

"Charlie," she cried, her cheek paling, "what— what was Rupert consulting you about?"

"Don't be alarmed, Milly, love," he answered, taking his boy upon one arm and putting the other about her waist.

"I have thought for some time that Rupert was growing thin and haggard," she said brokenly, tears filling her eyes," and—"Oh, Charlie, I have often noticed, and heard it remarked, that one death in a family is apt to follow closely upon another."

She ended with a sob, laying her head on his shoulder.

"Don't ky, mamma," cooed little Percy, patting her cheek; "oo baby boy tiss oo, make oo all well."

She lifted her head, returned the caresses lavished upon her by both husband and child, then asked earnestly and half pleadingly, "won't you tell me if—if Rupert is seriously ill?"

"He is broken down with overwork, has been devoting himself too closely to business, and needs an entire change for a time," replied her husband, speaking in a cheerful tone. "If he will take that at once and for a long enough time, he may, I think, be restored to full health and vigor."

"Surely, surely he will do so without delay?"

"I can't say. He thinks it almost impossible to leave his business at present and would rather try halfway measures first."

"He must be persuaded out of that, and I think can be," she said, her countenance brightening.

"Now you must excuse me for a few minutes, my dear. Gretchen is improving, but I cannot yet trust her to bake your waffles quite to my mind."

"Let her try, Milly. How else is she ever to learn?"

"I shall after I have seen that the iron is properly heated and filled," she answered, as she hastened away to the kitchen.

Celestia Ann was at the front gate as Rupert neared it. She turned her head at the sound of his footsteps.

"So here you be at last!" she exclaimed; "and I was lookin' right in the wrong direction. Been up to the doctor's, I s'pose? Well, they're set down to the table without ye. We waited a spell, an' then I told yor mother t'want no use, fer ye don't eat nothin' nohow, let me fix up the victuals good's I can."

"I am late, and sorry if the meal has been kept waiting," Rupert answered as he hurried past her into the house.

His mother gave him a kindly affectionate smile as he entered the dining room, and stopped his apology halfway.

"Never mind, my son, it is no matter, except that your meal will not, I fear, be quite so good and enjoyable, which is a pity, as your appetite is so poor of late."

There was some anxiety in her look and tone, also in the glance his father gave him as he seated himself at the table.

"I fear you are working too hard, Rupert," he said; "confining yourself too closely to business."

"Just what Charlie has been telling me," the

young man responded with a half-sigh. "But how is it to be helped?"

"By putting health before business," his mother said with decision. "My dear boy, if you lose your health, what will become of your business?"

"True, mother," he sighed, "but I have not quite given up the hope that I may regain the one without relinquishing the other."

"A pound of prevention is worth an ounce of cure," remarked Aunt Wealthy absently, rather as if thinking aloud than addressing the company.

"What does Charlie advise?" asked Mrs. Keith.

"An entire change for some months or a year, including a journey to some distant point. Quite impracticable, is it not, father?" Rupert asked, turning to him.

"If you want my opinion," replied Mr. Keith, "I say nothing is impracticable which is necessary to the preservation of your life or even of your health. We cannot spare you, my son," he continued with emotion. "It is to you more than any of the others that your mother and I look as the prop and support of our old age."

"Thank you, father," Rupert said with feeling. "That pleasing task would, of course, naturally fall to me as the eldest son, though if I were taken away, my brothers, I am sure, would be no less glad to undertake it."

"No, it would be the greatest joy in life," said Don with warmth, glancing affectionately from one to the other of his parents. "I can answer for Cyril as well as myself."

"I haven't the least doubt of it, Don," replied his father, while the mother said, with glistening eyes, "We are rich in the affection of our children, both boys and girls," she added, with a loving look into Annis's blue eyes.

The eyes filled with tears. Annis was thinking how often she had heard Fan say that she was to be the one always to stay at home and take care of father and mother. Dear Fan, who had now been nearly two months in heaven.

Oh, how they all missed her at every turn, though Annis strove earnestly to supply her place.

Leaving the table, they all repaired to the sitting room, but Don, after lingering a moment, took up his cap and moved toward the hall door.

"Don't forsake us, Don," said his mother, following his movements with a look of mingled love and sadness. It was no secret to her that the house seemed to him unbearably desolate, deprived of the loved presence of his favorite sister.

"Only for a few minutes, mother. I want a chat with Wallace, and this is about the best time to catch him at leisure."

"My poor boy!" sighed Mrs. Keith as the door closed on him.

"Yes, he feels very sad and lonely," said Rupert. "But I am glad he has left us for a little while, for I want to have a talk with you and father about him—myself also," he added, with a faint smile. "Don't go, Aunt Wealthy," he said as Miss Stanhope rose as if to leave the room. "What I have to say need be no secret from you, and I think we will all be glad of your counsel in the matter."

She sat down again, and Annis asked, "May I stay too, Rupert?"

"Yes," he said, inviting her to a seat by his side.

He then proceeded to give an account of his interview with Dr. Landreth, stating that he strongly advised him to wind up his business, or make some sort of arrangement for leaving it for a year or more, and join a party preparing for California. The journey across the plains he thought would prove the very thing for him. Nothing else was so likely to restore his shattered health."

"And I have been thinking," added Rupert, "that it might be the very best thing for Don if you, father and mother, would consent to let him go with me, in case I follow Charlie's advice. He seems to me as ill mentally as I am physically, and we would be mutual helpers.

"I have no idea that we should make our fortunes at gold digging, but I doubt if the boy will ever be content till he has tried his hand at it. But let his dreams be dispelled, and he will be ready to settle down at home."

"If he ever gets home again," remarked the father. "It may be that you are right, though, Rupert, and your mother and I will take the matter into consideration."

"Yes, sir, in regard to us both, I hope. I want your advice as to my own course; it will go far to help me decide what I ought to do."

Both parents looked gratified, while Miss Stanhope remarked, "You are quite right in that, Rupert. You could not have wiser counselors than they, and certainly none so deeply interested in your welfare. Nor will you, or anyone, ever lose by honoring parents."

"I am very fortunate in having parents worthy of all honor, Aunt Wealthy," he said with an affectionate glance from one to the other. "Mother, dear, do not look so sad," he said, perceiving that her eyes were full of tears. "I cannot think of going, if it is to be at the risk of breaking your heart."

"No, my heart will not break," she said in a determinately cheerful tone. "The promise is sure, 'As thy days, so shall thy strength be.' And it will be better to part with you for a time than forever in this life," she added with a tremble in her voice. "Also I should be more willing to see two of my boys go together than any one of them alone."

"Then if I go, you will consent to Don's accompanying me?"

"Yes."

"And you, father?"

"I feel just as your mother does about it," was Mr. Keith's reply.

"But if Don should not wish to go?" suggested Miss Stanhope in a tone of inquiry.

"Oh, no fear of that, auntie," laughed Annis. "He's been crazy to go ever since the first news of the gold, and you can't scare him out of it, either. The more you talk of Indians, bears, and wolves, and all other dangers, the more he wants to try it. He says life in this little slow town is altogether too tame to suit a fellow of spirit."

"Better suited to the humdrum class represented by his father and older brother, I presume," said Rupert with a good humored smile.

As Don stepped in at Wallace Ormsby's gate, Zillah opened the front door, ran out, and hastily caught up little Stuart, who was digging in the sand, and carried him struggling and screaming into the house.

"It's too cold for you to be out. Mamma can't let you. Mamma told you not to go out," she was saying as Don followed her into the sitting room.

"I will doe out! Ope de door!" screamed the child. "Me wants pay in de sand."

"No, you can't go out anymore tonight," replied the mother, giving him a hug and kiss. "Oh, he's mamma's darling! There never was such a boy in all the world—there never was! Mamma loves him ever so much."

Meanwhile, the child was struggling with all his baby might to get away from her, kicking, striking, screaming at the top of his voice, "I will doe out! *I will! I will!* Shan't 'tay in de house!"

"Oh, now, be a dear good boy," entreated Zillah. "He's mamma's own pet, the dearest, sweetest boy in the world. Mamma thinks there never was such a boy!"

"I should hope not, if that's the way he carries on," remarked Don, seating himself and regarding his nephew with a look of disgust and disapproval. "I think he's spoiling for a spanking, and if he were my child, he'd get it."

Zillah flushed hotly. "Men and boys have no patience with children," she said. "There, there, Stuart, stop crying and mamma will get you something good."

"No! Ope door! Me want doe out; me *will* doe out!" screamed the child.

"Oh, now, do be good. Do stop crying, and mamma will get you some candy," said Zillah in her most coaxing tones.

"Tanny, mamma?" asked the child, the screams suddenly ceasing and smiles breaking through the tears.

"Yes," Zillah said, drying his eyes and kissing him fondly, then rising with him in her arms and going to a cupboard.

But the size of the piece she offered did not suit the ideas of the young tyrant. He refused to accept it, and bursting into screams again, he demanded a bigger one.

"Take this in one hand, and you shall have a bigger piece in the other," said the over-indulgent mamma. And peace being restored, she sat down with him on her lap and began talking with Don.

"Where's Wallace?" the latter presently inquired.

"He went downtown again after tea but said he wouldn't be gone very long. Do you want to see him particularly?"

"I would like a talk with him," Don said with a sigh. "I wish he would try to get father and mother to consent to my joining the party that are going to California."

"Oh, Don, how can you suggest such a thing now when they are feeling so sad over poor Fan?" exclaimed Zillah, tears starting to her eyes.

"Don't think me hardhearted or wanting in love for them," Don returned with feeling, "but the truth is, I don't know how to endure life here now that Fan's gone. I miss her at every turn. I think it would be different in a new place where I had not been accustomed to her sweet society." His words were almost inaudible from emotion as he concluded.

"I know," Zillah said in trembling tones. "We all miss heer sadly, but I suppose it must be harder, perhaps, for you than any of the rest. Still you will soon grow in a measure used to it, no doubt. I have always heard that time assuages the bitterness of grief."

"I can't believe it, I don't believe it!" he cried impatiently. "At least I am sure it will not be so in my case for years, unless I can get away into new scenes that will help me to forgetfulness."

At that instant Stuart, who had got down from his mother's lap to play about the room, tripped and fell to the floor, striking his head against a chair.

He set up a loud scream, and Zillah ran to the rescue, picking him up with a cry of "Oh, poor darling, mamma is so sorry! Oh, it is just dreadful how many falls he gets! But there, never mind; it was a naughty chair that hurt my baby so. We'll give it a good whipping," she said, striking it with her hand several times as she spoke.

Stuart ceased screaming to pound the chair energetically with his tiny doubled-up fist, then consented to be bribed into quiet with another piece of candy.

Zillah sat down again with him on her lap, and presently he dropped asleep there.

"He ought to be in bed," remarked Don.

"Yes, but he didn't want to go, and I do so hate to have a battle with him."

"I rather think it will have to come to that sooner or later," said Don, "and I should think the longer you put it off, the harder it will be. I've been at Milly's a good deal the last few weeks, besides watching her when she was at home with us, and I think she could give you some valuable hints about managing a child."

"It is a vast deal easier to talk than to act, I can tell you, Don," was Zillah's half-offended retort.

"I daresay. But people can act as well as talk. Father and mother did with us—we always had to obey, and that without being petted and wheedled into it—and Milly does, too."

"I think it's a great deal better to coax than to beat them," Zillah said half angrily.

"Circumstances alter cases," said Don. "I don't think it's just the thing to pet and fondle a child, and tell him he's 'a darling; there never was such a boy,' and all that, when he's kicking up a row just because he isn't allowed to do exactly as he pleases. Percy began that very behavior the other evening when he had to go into the house before he considered it quite time."

"Well, what did Milly do with him?" inquired Zillah with some curiosity.

"She first told him firmly and quietly that he must stop screaming on the instant, or she would shut him in a room by himself till he was ready to be good. And as she always keeps her word, not threatening over and over again before she acts, as some people do, he did stop promptly. Then she took him on her lap and amused him with stories and rhymes a little while, when she carried him off to bed.

"She's always gently with him but firm as a rock. As regular as clockwork, too. He's put to bed when the hour comes and left there to go to sleep by himself, and he does it without a whimper."

"I suppose that's the orthodox way," said Zillah, "but I can't bear to force Stuart to bed when he cries to stay up. The sweet darling, I do love him so!" she said, bending down to kiss the round rosy cheek.

"I've no doubt you do," said Don, "but I remember to have heard mother say it was but a poor selfish kind of love that couldn't bear the pain of controlling a child for its own good but would rather let it become so willful and ill-behaved as to be a torment to itself and everybody else. Ah, here comes Wallace," he added, glancing from the window.

"Then I'll leave you to have your talk with him while I put this boy to bed," returned Zillah, rising and leaving the room.

Wallace was no sooner seated than Don made known his errand.

Wallace looked grave. "I don't like the idea, Don," he said. "I wish you could be persuaded to give it up. If you should be unsuccessful, of which there are ten chances to one, it would involve the loss of some of the best years of your life."

"One must take a risk in anything one tries," interrupted Don, impatiently.

"True," replied Wallace, "but in this more than in many others."

"'Nothing venture, nothing have,'" muttered Don.

"I thought you were to go to college in the fall," remarked Wallace.

"That has been father's plan for me, but as I have no fancy for a profession, I think a college course would be almost time thrown away—

money, too. Ru has proposed to make a druggist of me, but that isn't to my fancy, either."

"I wish you would go in with Ru, if you are determined not to take a collegiate education. I can see that he, poor fellow, is sadly overworked, and to have a brother in with him—one whom he could trust—would doubtless prove a great relief."

"Ru hasn't seemed well of late," assented Don in a reflective tone, "but I was laying it all to—to grief. Wallace, the house isn't what it used to be. I've thought I couldn't stand it. I've been a selfish dog, but I'll try to forget self and think of other people. Good evening. I promised mother I'd be back soon," he added, as he rose and took his departure.

His heart was filled with grief and disappointment. He crossed the street slowly, with head bent and eyes on the ground, battling earnestly with himself, striving to put aside his own inclinations for the sake of others.

He found the family still gathered in the sitting room, Dr. Landreth and Mildred with them.

As he entered, the doctor was saying to Rupert, "I have been considering your objections to my plans for you, and think I can see a way out of the difficulty in regard to leaving your business."

"What is that?" Rupert asked, and Don, aroused to eager interest, dropped into a chair and listened for the doctor's explanation with bated breath. "Could it be that Rupert was going from home? And if so, where? And what difference might it make in his own plans?"

"Simply this," returned Dr. Landreth with his genial smile, "that I will take charge of it and carry it on for you, if that arrangement seems to you entirely satisfactory."

"A most generous offer, Charlie!" exclaimed Rupert, flushing with surprise and gratitude, "but would it not interfere with your professional duties?"

"No, not necessarily. I should merely take the oversight, keeping the good clerk you have and getting another equally competent—the two to do the work between them."

"Many thanks," said Rupert, grasping his brother-in-law's hand. "You have removed my greatest difficulty. I begin to think I can follow out your prescriptions, if"—and he turned smilingly to Don—"if Don is as ready to sacrifice himself for my sake."

"I hope so, Ru. What is it?" the boy asked, a trifle huskily, for his momentary gleam of hope died out at the question.

It shone out with tenfold brilliancy at his brother's reply. "Charlie thinks I am in danger of permanent loss of health unless I give up my business for a time and have an entire change of scene, so he advises me to join the party about starting for California. He thinks the journey across the plains just the thing for me. But I ought to have some friend—say, a brother—with me, so it may depend upon your willingness to go."

"My willingness?" interrupted Don eagerly. "I'd be delighted, Ru, and do the very best for you that I know how."

The mother was regarding them with glistening eyes, her lips quivering with emotion.

"And let him give you the care and oversight an

elder brother should?" asked the father gravely.

"Yes, if he doesn't try to exert more than his rightful share of authority," returned Don, a slight reluctance perceptible in his tone.

"On that condition, your mother and I consent to your going," Mr. Keith said, "though, my boy, it will be hard indeed for us to part with you, our youngest son."

Don saw the tears in his mother's eyes, noted that his father's tones were not quite steady, and his heart went out in love to both. "I will never, never do anything to cause them shame or grief on my account," was the firm resolve he whispered to himself.

There was necessity for a speedy decision, and it was arrived at within twenty-four hours. The young men were to go. The allotted time was short for needed preparation, particularly that which fell to the mother's share. But with her three remaining daughters and Miss Stanhope coming to her assistance, and all working with a will, the thing was done well and quickly, nothing forgotten, nothing overlooked that could add to the comfort of the beloved travellers.

And it was well for all that matters were so hurried, leaving no leisure for sad forebodings or unavailing regrets.

The parting was a hard one, almost harder, the mother thought, than the last she had been called to pass through, for while her beloved Fan was safe from all sin and sorrow and suffering, these dear ones were to be exposed to many dangers and temptations.

But she bore up wonderfully as she bade them

adieu and watched the slow-moving train out of sight. They were not going beyond the reach of prayer. They would still be under the protecting care of Him who has said, "Behold, I am with thee, and will keep thee in all places whither thou goest, and will bring thee again into this land; for I will not leave thee, until I have done that which I have spoken to thee of."

"Wherever they might be, He would cover their defenseless heads with the shadow of His wing."

Annis's tears fell much longer and faster than her mother's. The letter she wrote to Elsie, giving a graphic account of the preparations and departure, was all blistered with them, even more so than the one telling of Fan's last hours.

"I am the only child left at home now," she wrote. "That was what mother said when we got back from seeing the long train of wagons with their ox teams starting on that long, dangerous journey. She took me in her arms and cried over me for a few minutes; then she wiped away her tears and kissed me over and over, saying, 'But we won't murmur, darling, or make ourselves unhappy about it, for they are all in God's good keeping. And one day, I trust, we shall all meet in that better land where partings are unknown.'

"And I have great reason to be thankful that Mildred and Zillah are so near us. It is almost as if they were still at home."

The letter wound up with an earnest request to Elsie that she would pray daily for the safe return of Rupert and Don.

CHAPTER NINTH

A child left to himself bringeth his mother to shame.

—PROVERBS 29:15

MAY HAD COME again, waking the flowers with her sunny skies and balmy breath, and our friends at Pleasant Plains spent much of their time in their gardens. Delighting in each other's society, they were often together, now in Mr. Keith's grounds, now in Dr. Landreth's, and later in Wallace Ormsby's.

Mrs. Keith missed her sons, who had always relieved her of the heavy part of the work of cultivating the flowers she so loved. But their place was filled, so far as that was concerned, by a hired gardener, and she found herself better able to endure the absence of Rupert and Don out of doors than in, especially when her daughters and baby grandsons were her companions.

Mildred took great pleasure in the laying out and improvement of the comparatively extensive grounds about her home, and husband, mother, aunt, and sisters entered heartily into her plans, helping with advice and suggestions—sometimes followed, sometimes not, but always appreciated—as evidence of their affectionate interests.

As for her husband, she and all her doings were altogether perfect in his eyes. She was queen of his small realm and could do no wrong. She excelled every other woman as wife, mother, and housekeeper; her taste was beyond criticism, and whatever she desired must be done.

He was nearly as great a paragon in her eyes, except as regarded the training of their child, to whom he would have shown unlimited indulgence if she could have seen it without remonstrance. That she could not, knowing how ruinous it would be; but her disapproval was never manifested before Percy. She would not have him know or suspect that his parents differed in regard to his training.

And, indeed, it was only when she and Charlie were quite alone that she addressed him on the subject, never in an unkind, fault-finding way but with gentle persuasion and arguments drawn from observation and the teachings of Scripture.

Loving the child with an affection even deeper and tenderer than his, she was yet much more disposed to curb and restrain where she saw it to be for his good. Her sense of parental responsibility was far stronger than the father's, and while he looked upon Percy as, for the present at least, scarcely more than a pretty babe, she regarded the child as a sacred trust, a little immortal whose welfare for time and eternity might depend largely upon her faithfulness in right training and teaching.

"My dear Milly, he is so young, such a mere baby," the doctor would sometimes say, "that it can't do him much harm to get his own way for a

while. It will be time enough a year or two hence
to begin his education."

"A very great mistake," Mildred would answer
gravely. "I have had a good deal to do with young
children, and am convinced that a child's education begins as soon as it knows its mother's voice
and can note the changing expression of her
countenance. And, Charlie, it is far easier to learn
than to unlearn. If we let our child acquire bad
habits at the start, it will be a far more difficult
task to break them up and substitute good ones
than to train him to such in the very beginning."

Zillah was quite as devoted a wife and competent a housekeeper as her older sister but not so
wise and faithful a mother. No child was more
comfortably or tastefully clad than hers or had
more tender caresses lavished upon it. She meant
also to take proper care of his bodily health and
was quite resolved in the long run to train him in
the way he should go. She wanted him to grow up
a good man and a strong and healthy one, but in
the meantime she was often weakly indulgent, to
the damage of both his physical and moral natures.

The two sisters, taking work and babies along,
were spending a sociable afternoon with their
mother.

The little boys, playing about the room, met
with an occasional mishap.

Percy tripped on the carpet and fell, striking
his head against the leg of the table.

He burst into a cry, and Annis, running to pick
him up, exclaimed, "Oh, the poor little dear! That
did hurt him, I know."

But Mildred, taking him from her, said in a

sprightly tone, "Oh, he's mother's soldier boy; he isn't going to cry for a trifle. But what a blow the table got! Poor table!" And she bent down and stroked and patted it pityingly.

Percy stopped crying to echo her words and imitate her action. "Percy didn't doe to hurt oo. Percy tiss the p'ace and mate it well," he went on, suiting the action to the word.

Then his mother having dried his eyes and given him a kiss, he went back to his play.

Zillah had watched the scene with interest.

"Is that the way you do?" she said to Mildred. "Don told me that was your way, and I believe, as he says, it is better than mine."

"What is yours?" asked Mildred, resuming the sewing she had dropped on Percy's fall.

"Oh, I've always made a fuss over my boy's hurts, pitied him, and blamed the chair or table or whatever he had struck against for hurting him, and have pretended to punish it, just to take his attention from his hurt and so stop his crying."

"Are you not afraid of teaching him to be selfish and revengeful?" Mildred asked with a look of grave concern.

"I never thought of that, and am afraid it may," said Zillah frankly. "I shall not do so any more."

Annis was entertaining her little nephews and presently came with a request. "The boys want me to take them out to the garden to play horse. May I?"

"I have no objection to Percy's going," said Mildred. "The fresh air will be very good for him, I think, as well as the exercise."

"But I don't want Stuart to go," Zillah said.

"He has a bad cold and ought to be kept in the house. Slip away from him if you can, Annis, for if he sees you and Percy start out, he'll scream himself sick. Or if not himself, other people," she added with a laugh.

"I'll do my best, but you will have to engage his attention for a while," said Annis.

"Yes. Stuart, come here; mamma wants to speak to you."

"No! Me's doin' out, p'ay horse wis Percy," the child returned with a scowl and a shake of his little shoulders.

Zillah put down her sewing, rose, and went to him. "Come with mamma," she said in coaxing tones, stooping down to caress him. "Don't you want to go out to the kitchen and see what Celestia Ann is doing?"

"No, me don't. Me's doin' outdoors to p'ay horse wis Percy!" shouted the child defiantly, quite seeing through the artifice.

Zillah began to grow impatient. "No, you are not," she said peremptorily. "You cannot play out of doors at all today because you have a bad cold, and it would make you sick."

"I will! I will! I will!" screamed the child, stamping his foot at her and clenching his tiny fist. "Ope de door dis minute, naughty mamma. I will doe out p'ay horse."

There was something comical in his baby rage, and unfortunately Zillah could not refrain from laughing, though the other ladies looked on in grave concern.

Her mirth had not a happy effect upon the little rebel. Bursting from her grasp, he ran toward

the door just closing on Annis and Percy, screaming at the top of his voice, "Let me doe wis you,
Annis! Ope de door," pounding on it with his
fists, then taking hold of the knob and trying to
turn it for himself.

"You bad boy, I'm ashamed of you," Zillah said,
taking his hand, which he instantly snatched away.
"Stop this screaming, or I'll take you home."

"No! Shan't doe home. Me's doin' out p'ay
horse wis Percy."

"I do believe he's the most persistent child I
ever saw or that ever was made!" Zillah
exclaimed with angry impatience, apparently
addressing the company in general. "I wonder if
it would hurt him to go out for a little while if I
wrap him up well. Do you think it would,
mother?"

"Perhaps not physically, Zillah," Mrs. Keith
answered with look and tone of grave disapproval, "but morally it certainly would have a
very bad effect. You have told him positively that
he shall not go out to play today, and if you break
your word, how can you expect him ever to
esteem his mother a perfectly truthful woman?"

"You make a very serious matter of it, mother,"
Zillah said, reddening.

"It is a very serious thing, my dear daughter,"
Mrs. Keith answered in her own sweet, gentle
way and with a look of loving sympathy.

She would have said more, but Stuart at that
instant renewed the screams he had ceased for a
moment upon perceiving symptoms of relenting
on his mother's part.

But Zillah now felt that for very shame she

must remain firm. She tried the old plan of coaxing and wheedling—offered picture books, stories, candy—but nothing would do except the forbidden pleasure, and at length, losing all patience, she took him into another room and gave him the punishment Don would have liked to prescribe on a former occasion. Then she cried over him while he sobbed himself to sleep in her arms.

Having laid him on a bed, covered him carefully, and left a tender kiss on his cheek, she went back to the sitting room where the others were.

Sitting down by her mother's side, she took up her sewing and tried to go on with it, but her hands trembled and tears dimmed her sight. She dropped the work to wipe them away.

"Oh, mother," she said in quivering tones, "what shall I do with that child? I can never bring him up right, as you have brought up all yours."

"It is a great work, dear, to train a child in the way he should go," Mrs. Keith answered in sympathizing tones. "And the wisest of us may well ask, 'Who is sufficient for these things?' yet rejoice and take courage in the assurance that 'our sufficiency is of God.' Do not forget His gracious promise, 'If any of you lack wisdom, let him ask of God, that giveth to all men liberally, and upbraideth not; and it shall be given him.'

"Whatever success I may have had in bringing up my children aright has been given me in answer to prayer and in fulfillment of that promise."

"I love him so dearly I can hardly bear to refuse him anything," sighed Zillah, wiping her eyes and resuming her work.

"I hope, daughter, that you love him well enough

to give yourself the pain of refusing him hurtful indulgences," was her mother's grave response. "It often requires deeper, truer love to deny than to grant, to punish than to let slip, but 'a child left to himself bringeth his mother to shame.'"

"Yes, mother, I know that is Bible truth, and I do not intend to leave mine to himself. I do really earnestly desire to bring him up for God and heaven, faulty as my training has been, I fear, thus far. But he is so young yet! It seems so hard to discipline such a mere baby."

"I know it does, my dear child — I have not forgotten my own experience — but I assure you, you will spare much suffering to both him and yourself by beginning early the lesson that parental authority is to be respected and prompt and cheerful obedience rendered.

"Be very gentle with him, giving your directions in the form of requests rather than commands, unless it becomes necessary to order him. I think children should be treated with consideration and politeness as well as grown people. It is the best way to teach them to be polite and considerate toward others."

"It was your way of teaching us, mother," remarked Mildred with an affectionate, smiling glance into her mother's sweet, placid face.

"And a very effectual one it has proved in their case," remarked Miss Stanhope.

"I think it has," said Mrs. Keith. Then she went on: "There is another thing, my two dear daughters, that I wish to impress upon you: It is the paramount importance of always keeping your word with your children. Try not to make hasty promises or threats, which you may regret having to carry out, but having once passed your word, let nothing induce you to be false to it.

"I need scarcely urge upon you the importance of being always entirely truthful with them, since you know how severely the Scriptures condemn any, even the slightest, departure from truth."

"I should hope not, indeed, mother," said Zillah. "I know I have not always been firm with my boy, have sometimes let him gain his wishes — which I have at first denied — by persistent fretting and crying, and have often coaxed when I ought to have demanded obedience. But I have never tried to secure his obedience by deceiving or telling him what was not true."

"It is surprising what very lax ideas many persons — yes, even some who profess to be Christians — have in regard to that thing," remarked Miss Stanhope. "Shrinking from the exertion or the pain of enforcing obedience by legitimate means, they resort to subterfuge, prevarication, or even downright falsehood.

"I have heard a mother say to her refractory or crying child, 'If you don't come into the house now, a big black bear will catch you,' or 'If you don't stop that screaming, a dog will come and bite you.'

"Besides that, they will utter threats they have not the remotest intention of carrying out, a fact which the little ones are not slow to discover and act upon."

At this point the conversation was interrupted by a call from two neighbors. It was of a most unfashionable length, and the talk ran principally upon housekeeping, children, and servants.

One of the callers, an elderly lady, had several little anecdotes to tell of the smart sayings and doings of her grandchildren, one of them so aptly illustrating Miss Stanhope's recent remarks that Mildred and Zillah could not refrain from a furtive exchange of significant glances. This was the narrative that drew them forth.

"Two of my grandchildren were staying at our house last week, Mary Bronson, my son's daughter—she's ten years old—and Tommy Linn, my oldest daughter's child—he's about five and has a great notion of being a man. He's out of petticoats now, and you couldn't punish him worse than by making him put them on again.

"Well, the second night he was with us, I was in a quandary. His nightgown had been hung out to air, and a shower had come up and made it soaking wet, for you see, nobody had thought to bring it in, and his mother had sent only one.

"When Tommy saw the condition it was in, he spoke right up: 'Grandmother, don't you give me a girl's nightgown, 'cause I shan't wear it. I want to have a man's.'

"'Yes,' I said, 'so you shall. Mary, you go and get one of his Uncle Sam's for him.' Then I whispered to her, 'Bring one of yours.'

"So she brought it, and as I shook it out, Tommy looked at it very suspiciously. 'Is that a man's?' he says.

"'Yes,' says I, 'it's one of your Uncle Sam's.' So he let me put it on him and went off to sleep as quiet and contended as could be."

"But do you think it was right?" asked Miss Stanhope in a tone of gentle remonstrance. "It was not the truth you told the child."

"No," acknowledged Mr. Bronson reluctantly, "but what is a body to do? You have to manage children somehow, and if I hadn't deceived him, there'd have been a regular battle. What would you have done in my place?"

"Anything, I hope, rather than tell an untruth to one child and give a lesson in falsehood and deception to the other. Excuse an old woman's plain speaking, but how can you ever tell that little Mary that lying is a great sin — a sin that must cost the loss of the soul if unrepented of and unforsaken? Or how blame her if she, at some future day, puts your lesson in practice to deceive you, perchance in some matter of vital importance to you or herself?"

There was silence in the room for some moments, while Mrs. Bronson sat looking extremely uncomfortable. Then she said, with an attempt to speak lightly, "You make a very serious matter of it, Miss Stanhope."

"It is a serious matter," returned Aunt Wealthy, "as I am sure you will acknowledge upon thoughtful consideration. I am sorry to cause you mental disquiet, but 'faithful are the wounds of a friend,' the wise man says."

"That is true, and I daresay you are right. I shall think over what you have been saying," Mrs. Bronson returned, rising to take leave.

"What do you think of it all?" she asked her companion as they left the house.

"I'm afraid the old lady was right, Sarah,

though I confess I never thought of it in that light before—telling fibs to children to keep them from misbehaving, I mean. I've done it occasionally myself, but I don't think I ever shall again. As she said, how can we expect them to speak the truth if we are not always careful to do it ourselves?"

"Annis," Mildred called to her sister, "please bring Percy in now. It is growing too late for him to be out."

"He doesn't want to come," was the answer. "Can't he stay out a little longer?"

"No, the sun is near setting, and the air is growing quite cold," Mildred answered, running down into the garden and taking her little boy by the hand. "Come, son, we must go in now, for mamma does not want her dear baby to get sick."

"No, won't get sick," he asserted in the most positive manner. "P'ease, mamma, let Percy tay wee 'ittle bit longer."

"No, darling, but if it is a good day tomorrow, you shall have a nice long play and a drive in the carriage with papa and mamma, besides."

She was leading him gently on toward the house while she spoke. The child did not resist, but he set up a loud wail.

"My little boy must not be naughty," Mildred said in a gently reproving tone.

Still, the crying continued and indeed increased in violence as she led him over the threshold into the hall. There she stopped, and stooping down to take off his outdoor garments, she said firmly, "Percy, you must stop this noise at once. Mamma is very sorry her little boy is so naughty. Now be good, and we will go into the parlor to see dear grandma and the rest, and you may get up on a chair by the window and watch for grandpa, and papa, and Uncle Wallace to come to supper. They'll be coming pretty soon, and then we will have our supper, and after that Percy shall go to his nice little bed."

Being of a pleasant disposition, and having already learned by experience that nothing was ever gained from his mother by fretting, crying, or teasing, the little fellow presently ceased his wailing, allowed her to dry his eyes, gave her a kiss and a promise to be good, and was so for the rest of his stay at this grandfather's.

Zillah had watched the little scene with interest and had not failed to note the fact that Don's report of Mildred's management was correct. She did not caress and hug her child while he was misbehaving but treated him in a way to make it evident to him that his conduct was displeasing to her.

At the tea table there was again an illustration of the difference in the training the two children were receiving. Percy was given only plain, wholesome food suited to his infant years. Stuart, refusing to be content with that, was permitted to eat cake, preserves, meat—in fact, everything upon the table to which he chose to take a fancy.

"Is that the way you feed your child?" the doctor asked in a tone of surprise quite unmingled with approval.

"Yes," replied Wallace carelessly, "he eats whatever we do. We let him have anything on the table that he fancies. You don't think it the best plan, I see."

"No, unless your object is to make an invalid of him."

"I couldn't bear to eat dainties without giving my child a share!" exclaimed Zillah with some heat. "And it never hurts him."

"I think you are mistaken there," said the doctor. "That such indulgence does not immediately result in violent illness is no proof that it does no harm. I am afraid you will discover one day, when it is too late, that very serious harm has been done. There is great danger that his digestive organs will give way under the great strain put upon them, and if you do not lose him, you will have him a sufferer for life."

Zillah looked startled and alarmed, and Wallace, turning to her, said, "If that's the case, little wife, we must promptly turn over a new leaf with him. I'm afraid Charlie has the right of it. You know how restless Stuart is often at night, and I daresay it's all owing to our foolish habit of indulging him in eating rich and unwholesome food."

"I suppose so. I begin to think I am not fit to have a child," Zillah said half impatiently, half sadly, "for my management so far seems to have been all blunders."

"Live and learn, daughter," her father said cheerily. "Don't be disheartened, but set about correcting your mistakes as fast as possible. I don't think," he added, patting Stuart's head, "that my namesake grandson is quite ruined yet. Do you, Uncle Charlie?"

"Oh no, indeed!" replied the doctor. "He's a fine little fellow, and I want him to have a chance to continue such, physically as well as otherwise."

"It shall not be his father's fault if he doesn't," said Wallace.

"Nor his mother's," added Zillah. "Wallace, we would rather live on very plain fare ourselves than have our boy injured with rich living, wouldn't we?"

"Certainly; but perhaps that need not be the only alternative," he answered with a good-humored smile.

"I'm sure I don't want to have a battle with him at every meal," she said disconsolately.

"Perhaps that may be avoided by sending him to his play before bringing on objectionable dishes," said her husband.

Chapter Tenth

Elsie and her Brother

"Horace, bring papa that newspaper that lies on the table yonder," Mr. Dinsmore said to his little son.

The child, seated in his own little chair by his mother's side, was listlessly turning the pages of a picture book. Elsie had just finished her recitations for the morning and was now sitting on the other side of Rose, taking a lesson in fancy work.

Mr. Dinsmore had spoken in a pleasant tone, rather of request than command, yet Horace, though usually ready to obey promptly and cheerfully, sat perfectly still, as if he had not heard or did not choose to heed.

"Horace, do you hear me? Go and bring me that paper," said his father, and this time the tone was one of stern command.

The child's face instantly assumed a stubborn, sullen expression, while he neither moved nor answered.

Elsie, pale and trembling with apprehension, gave him an entreating, her father an imploring look, which neither seemed to see.

Mr. Dinsmore was regarding his son with a

look of stern displeasure, and Horace's eyes were on his book.

"Horace, dear, do as papa bids you," said Rose with gentle entreaty.

"Leave him to me, Rose," said her husband. "I have given the order, and I am the one to enforce it. Horace, obey me instantly or I shall whip you till you do."

At that stern sentence, Elsie almost cried out in fear and dismay, for well she knew her father's indomitable will, and she could perceive that Horace, whom she so dearly loved that to see him suffer pain was far worse than to have it inflicted upon herself, was just now in a most stubborn, refractory mood.

Probably the state of the atmosphere had something to do with it, for it was a rainy day, close and sultry.

"Me don't want to," muttered the little fellow, making no movement to obey. Then, as he felt a not very gentle grasp upon his arm, he cried, "Me won't!" and cast a defiant look upon his father's face.

Mr. Dinsmore instantly administered a pretty severe chastisement, Rose sitting by pale and sad, Elsie with the tears streaming over her cheeks.

Horace cried violently but still refused obedience to the reiterated command, "Go and get that paper and bring it to me."

The punishment was repeated with added severity, but he stubbornly persisted in his refusal, and the battle went on till his mother, unable to endure the sight, rose and left the room, and Elsie so far forgot herself in her darling little brother's pain that she ran to the rescue, threw her arms about him, and tried to drag him away from her father.

"Oh, papa, don't!" she sobbed. "Please don't whip him any more! I cannot bear it."

"Elsie! How dare you!" Mr. Dinsmore exclaimed in astonishment and wrath, putting her forcibly aside as he spoke. "Leave the room instantly," he added in his sternest tones and with a stamp of his foot.

She let go her hold of the child, but, lingering, began again her entreaty, "Oh, papa, please—"

"Will you compel me to punish you in the same way?" he said, again stamping his foot and pointing significantly to the door.

At that she hastened from the room and sought her own, crying as if her heart would break.

Horace yielded at last, when nearly exhausted with the conflict, received a kiss of reconciliation from his father, was then carried to his mother, and wept himself to sleep in her arms, her tears falling almost as fast as his.

She had laid him in his crib and was bending over him, tenderly smoothing back the damp curls from his heated brow, when her husband came softly to here side and, putting his arm about her waist, asked in low, moved tones, "Do you blame me, my Rose? Do you think me a cruel father?"

She did not answer for a moment but seemed struggling with emotion.

He sighed deeply.

"I—I think you were conscientious in it all," she said in length, her voice tremulous with feeling, "and that after beginning the conflict it was necessary for you to conquer. But I think the beginning of it was a sad mistake."

"How do you mean? What would you have had me do when my child refused to obey a command so simple and easy to understand and do?"

"My husband," she said, allowing him to lead her to a sofa, where they sat down side by side, "I do not like to seem to try to teach you who are so much older and wiser than I. But do you not think you would have spared yourself and all of us a great deal of pain if instead of compelling obedience, you had simply punished refusal to obey, and there let the matter rest?"

"Would it have gone as far toward securing obedience in the future?" he queried, rather as if considering the question himself than asking her opinion.

"I think so," she said. "Surely a child will not be apt to disobey very often when he finds that swift punishment is always meted out in proportion to the magnitude of the offense."

He sat silently meditating for some little time, she anxiously watching the expression of his face.

At length, turning to her, he said, "I believe you are right, my love, and I shall, if possible, avoid such conflicts in the future, as you advise, simply punishing the act of disobedience or refusal to obey. Today that course would, as you have suggested, have saved us all a great deal of suffering. And oh, what would it not have saved to Elsie and myself if put into practice years ago!" He sighed deeply as he added, "And the pain occasioned by this unfortunate conflict is not all over yet, for I have her to punish now."

"Elsie?" exclaimed Rose, looking at him in great surprise. "What has she done?"

He told her what had occurred just as she left the room where he was battling with Horace, adding, "I must, of course, punish her, for she was not only rebelling against my authority herself but upholding her brother in doing the same."

"I suppose so," said Rose sadly, "but I wish you could feel it right and wise to forgive her."

"Not till I have inflicted some punishment," he said. "The offense was quite too serious to be lightly passed over."

"But you will not be severe with her?" Rose said pleadingly. "You know it was only her great love for her little brother that made her for a moment forgetful of her duty to you. And I am sure she is repenting bitterly now."

"I have no intention of inflicting corporal punishment, if that is what you apprehend," he said. "But I think I ought to make her aware, for a day or two at least, that she is in disgrace with me."

"I am so sorry," sighed Rose, "for though to some children that would be a very slight punishment, I know that to her it will be positively dreadful."

"Yes," he returned, echoing her sigh, "she is extravagantly fond of her father's caresses and endearments, but so is he of hers, and I doubt if the punishment will be more severe to the one than to the other of us."

"What's de mattah, chile? What's de mattah wid you an' little massa?" Aunt Chloe asked with an anxious, troubled look as Elsie rushed into her own apartments crying very bitterly.

Amid heavy sobbing and floods of tears, the little girl related what had passed between her father and brother, winding up with the story of her interference and its result.

"Oh, darlin' chile, dat was bad!" exclaimed Chloe. "You shouldn't neber do no sich ting as dat! Dat be bery bad ting fo' little massa, what you ben an' gone an' done. De Bible say chillens mus' min' dere fadder and mudder."

Elsie made no reply but threw herself on a couch and half buried her face in a pillow in the effort to shut out the sound of Horace's cries, which penetrated even there.

Until they ceased, she scarcely thought of anything but that he was being hurt. But when all grew quiet with the ending of the conflict, she was suddenly struck with the enormity of her offense and the dread certainty that her father was greatly and justly incensed at her unwarrantable interference between him and her brother.

She was astonished at her own temerity and trembled at thought of the probable consequences. That some sort of punishment would be meted out to her she had not the slightest doubt, and as her father was wont to be prompt in action, she fully expected a visit from him as soon as he was done disciplining Horace.

She listened with a quaking heart for the sound of his approaching footsteps, but the minutes and the hours crept on and he came not.

The dinner bell rang, and Elsie started up full of perplexity and alarm, doubting whether she was or was not expected to obey its summons.

"Oh, mammy," she cried, "I don't know what

to do! I don't want to go to the table. Please go and ask papa if I may be excused. Tell him my head aches, for indeed it does, and I'm not at all hungry."

"Co'se, chile, co'se you's got misery in de head after all dat cryin'," replied Aunt Chloe, putting down her knitting to go and do the errand. "Don' cry no mo', honey. Maybe massa forgib you, ef you's right down sorry."

"I am sorry, mammy," sobbed Elsie; "Oh, I am very sorry. But I know that papa will punish me somehow or other, and I deserve it."

"Maybe not, honey," responded Aunt Chloe cheerfully, then hurried away to the dining room.

She returned in a few minutes, bringing a very nice meal daintily arranged on a silver tray.

"What did papa say?" asked Elsie anxiously.

"Not much, honey, only, 'Bery well, Aunt Chloe, you kin take her something when she feels inclined to eat.'"

Elsie's tears burst forth afresh. Was it then a matter of indifference to her father that she was in pain? Her father, who was usually so full of loving anxiety at the slightest indication of anything being amiss with her?

"Oh, mammy," she sobbed, "what if papa shouldn't ever love me anymore!"

"Ki, chile, dat a heap ob nonsense you's talkin' now!" laughed Chloe. "Massa couldn't never help it, not a bit. You's jes' de light ob his eyes. Dere now, don' cry no mo', but jes' eat what your ole mammy fetch fo' you."

There was some slight and temporary comfort in the assurance her mammy expressed, and the little girl found herself able, by its help, to eat sparingly of the dainties she had brought her.

"Did papa say I must stay in my rooms till I got permission to leave them?" she asked.

"No, honey darlin', he didn't say nuffin' 't all 'bout dat. Didn't gib no corrections, but jes' 'bout gibin' you what you wants to eat when you's ready fo' it. Dat don' soun' so mighty bad fo' yo' case, chile, an' I respects mass'll be comin' in 'rectly fo' to kiss an' make up."

"No," Elsie said, shaking her head and bursting into tears again, "he'll punish me first. I am quite sure of that."

"Ki, chile! ef he gwine fo' to do dat, what you 'spose he waitin' fo'?"

"I don't know," sobbed the little girl, "but I'm afraid it will be a long while before he will hug and kiss me again, or give me a kind look or word."

"Why you tink dat, honey?"

"Oh, because he looked so stern and angry when he stamped his foot at me and ordered me out of the room."

The afternoon passed very slowly in the constant yet vain expectation of a visit from her father or a summons to his presence. Several times she was on the point of venturing into it without being called, but her heart failed her. She was not sure that it might not be looked upon as an additional offense, for he had sent her out of the room without saying how long he meant her banishment to last.

Besides, she wanted to be sure of seeing him alone. She would not have even Rose a witness of the interview.

So she waited till the hour when the latter would be engaged in seeing little Horace put to bed for the night, then in much trepidation went in search of her father. She felt quite sure of finding him alone, for there were no guests in the house, and as it was still storming, there seemed no danger of any one calling.

She went first to the parlor, which was their principal family room when alone. Yes, there he was, sitting in an easy chair by a window, his back toward her, doubtless reading and quite alone.

She stole noiselessly to the back of his chair, her heart beating very fast and loud. She almost thought he must hear it, but he seemed unaware of her approach, entirely absorbed in his book.

She caught hold of the chair back to steady and support herself, for she was trembling in every limb.

"Papa, I—" she began, her voice full of tears.

"I have nothing to say to you, Miss Dinsmore, except that I forbid you to address me by that title or to call me father or to take any liberties with me that would be unsuitable in a stranger guest in the house," he interrupted, in a freezing tone without turning toward her and with his eyes still upon his book.

"Oh, I can't bear it! I can't!" she cried with a burst of sobs and tears, throwing herself at his feet. "I know I've behave very badly, but I'm—"

"Get up," he said sternly, again interrupting her. "Control yourself or leave the room till you can."

His look was as stern and cold as his words.

She struggled to her feet and went back to her own rooms, crying very bitterly.

"Oh, mammy, mammy," she sobbed, "it's even worse than I expected, for I'm forbidden to call him father or papa. Oh, what shall I do? How can I call him anything else? And I mustn't hug or kiss him or sit on his knee. And—and he called me 'Miss Dinsmore.' Just think of it! Not even Elsie, without the pet names I love so to hear from his lips, but Miss Dinsmore, as if I were a stranger he cared nothing about."

"'Tain't gwine to las' long, honey darlin', dat ar ain't," said Chloe soothingly, taking the weeper in her arms and caressing her tenderly. "You jes' de light ob massa's eyes, like I tole you befo', an' de pet names be sho' to come again fo' long. 'Sides, you'll hab yo' ole seat on massa's knee an' all de hugs and kisses you wants."

"I'm afraid not for a long while, mammy," sobbed the little girl. "I think papa has not been so displeased with me since that dreadful time so long ago, when we lived at Roselands."

The tea bell rang.

"Is you gwine to de table, darlin'?" Chloe asked.

"Oh no, no, mammy!" Elsie exclaimed with a fresh burst of grief. "Papa bade me leave the room till I could control myself, and I know I could not do that in his presence yet. Oh, how can I ever be with him and not call him father or papa?"

As they sat down to the table, Rose glanced at the vacant seat, then at her husband. "I fear the dear child is ill with grief and remorse, Horace," she said with a troubled, anxious look. "She has such a tender conscience and so dearly loves the father whose displeasure she has incurred."

"She is not ill. I saw her a few moments ago," he answered with a sigh. "She is distressed, I know, but it is the consequence of her own wrongdoing, and she must endure it for a time that she may learn never again to encourage her brother in resistance to lawful authority."

"Don't you think the lesson may be already learned?" Rose said pleadingly. "She has no stubbornness in her nature but is very easily subdued and made penitent."

"I am not so sure of that. She comes of very stubborn stock, on one side at least," he replied with a rather melancholy attempt at pleasantry.

"My dear husband, I wish you would forgive her," pleaded the young stepmother. "Surely you will before she goes to bed tonight?"

"Can you not be content to leave her to me, my Rose?" he asked. "Do you not know that I am a most doting father? That she is the very light of my eyes, and core of my heart? Ah, I sometimes fear she is her father's idol."

"No," Rose said, half chokingly and with tears in her eyes, "I am sure your conscience need not trouble you on that score so long as you can find it in your heart to be so severe with her faults."

"Not in my heart, love," he returned, a little hurt, "but in the settled conviction that I am acting for her good. It requires a strong effort of my will to resist the promptings of affection, of love that urges me to send for her at once, tell her she is forgiven, and lavish the tenderest caresses upon her."

"That is just what I should rejoice to see you do," said Rose.

"Tomorrow or the next day, perhaps you may," he answered in a tone that seemed to imply that he wished to hear no more on the subject. And Rose, like the wise woman and affectionate wife that she was, dropped it, though her heart ached for Elsie.

After they had left the dining room for the parlor, she asked if she might go to the little girl's apartments and see if she were feeling quite well.

"I really don't like to claim so much authority over my wife as to forbid her going where she will about my house, which is her own also," he said with a slight smile, "but I should prefer to have the child left to herself for the present. I have not confined her to her rooms, and she can join us when she will. I only bade her leave my presence this afternoon till she could control herself, and she would understand from that that she was at liberty to return to it when ready to comply with the condition."

"How she will miss her good-night chat seated upon her father's knee, the good-night hug and kiss he has been wont to bestow upon her!" sighed Rose.

"Yes," he said, in a moved tone, rising and beginning to pace the room in a disturbed way, "she will hardly know what to do without them— nor shall I—but we must. Don't make any further efforts to shake my resolve, Rose, for I cannot, must not, pass lightly over so serious a misdemeanor as she has been guilty of in this instance."

Rose could but comply with his wishes, so plainly and strongly expressed, and Elsie passed the evening alone, except for the companionship of her nurse, for she dared not trust herself again in her father's presence till she could hope to be able to maintain the self-control he required.

As her hour for retiring drew near, Aunt Chloe noted how she was listening for approaching footsteps, at the same time glancing frequently at her watch or the clock on the mantle.

"Sho, honey, you's gwine to de parlor to say good night fo' you goes to bed?" she remarked inquiringly.

Elsie shook her head, the tears rolling down her cheeks. "How can I, mammy, when I mustn't say 'father' or 'papa'?" she sobbed. "I couldn't without crying, if at all, and papa forbade me his presence till I could control myself. There, my bedtime has come, and papa hasn't. Oh, I could hardly help hoping he did not mean to let me go to bed unforgiven. There's never been a night before since—since those dreadful days at Roselands, that I've gone without his kiss or without being held close to his heart with tender, loving words as if I were the dearest thing to him in all the world."

"Don't you go for to fret yo' po' heart out, blessed chile," Chloe said, taking her nursling in her kind arms. "Yo' ole mammy lubs you like her life; so does yo' pa, too. An' maybe he's gwine come in hyah 'bout de time you's ready fo' bed to kiss an' make up ef you promises neber to do so no mo' as you been an' gone an' done dis hyah mornin'."

"Oh no, never, never!" Elsie sobbed, hiding her face for a moment on Aunt Chloe's shoulder. "I don't know how I ever dared to do it! I deserve to be punished very severely. No wonder papa is so displeased with me."

She was soon in bed but did not, as usual with her, fall asleep at once. She lay for a good while listening to every sound, hoping even against hope that her father would relent and come to give her his forgiveness and a loving kiss while she slept. But he did not, and at length she cried herself to sleep. It was the same thing over again in the morning: She hoped he would come to her to inquire of her penitence and good resolutions for the future, or send for her to go to him. But she waited and wished in vain, breakfasted in her own rooms—still too distrustful of her power of self-control to venture to join her parents in the breakfast room—then prepared her tasks for the day, yet she could not find courage to carry them to her father that he might hear her recitations.

She was glad the weather continued such as to keep visitors away. She hoped none would come till this trouble of hers was over, for how could she bear to have any one out of the family—even good, kind Mr. Travilla—know that she had so displeased her father? And while his displeasure lasted, how impossible it would be for any guest to fail to perceive it.

She tried one employment after another— needlework, reading, music—but found no interest in any of them, and every now and then she would give way to a fit of violent weeping.

"Oh," she said to herself, "how long is it to last? Papa did not say, and I don't know when he will think I have been punished enough."

So the day wore wearily away, and night came again without any change for the better.

Sadly mourning over her estrangement from her father, and longing inexpressibly for his forgiveness and loving favor, a thought struck her.

"Ah, yes," she said half aloud, "I will write to papa the confession and plea for pardon he would not let me speak."

Opening her writing desk, she selected a sheet of paper, took up her pen, and dipped it in the ink. But, alas, how should she begin her note? By what title should she address the father who had forbidden her to call him that? How impossible to call him anything else! How disrespectful, how impertinent to omit a title altogether!

She laid down her pen, pushed the paper aside, and covering her face with her hand, wept long and bitterly, Chloe watching her with tear-dimmed eyes.

"Precious chile," she said at length, "what kin yo' ole mammy do fo' her pet?"

"Nothing, mammy, unless you could persuade my father to forgive and love me again."

"Po' dear, he'll do dat befo' long; I'se pow'ful sure ob dat. Massa so fond ob you he kain't hole out much longer hisself. Was you gwine write sumfin' to massa, honey?"

"Yes, but I can't because he forbade me to call him father or papa, and—and oh, I don't know how to call him anything else. Oh, mammy, I don't believe I can sleep at all tonight without his forgiveness!"

"Den 'spose my chile go an' ax massa fo' it."

"No, I dare not, because he forbade me to take

any greater liberty with him than a stranger guest might or to come into his presence till I could be calm, and I know I could not yet."

"Den yo' ole mammy gwine fo' you, an' dis am de bes' time, kase I 'spect massa by hisself in de parlor," she said, rising and leaving the room.

As she had expected, she found Mr. Dinsmore alone in the parlor. Dropping a curtsey, she stood before him with folded hands, waiting in respectful silence for an invitation to speak.

"Well, Aunt Chloe, what is it?" he asked.

"Massa, my chile frettin' herself sick."

"She must not do that," he said with a touch of sternness in his tone.

"Please, sah, s'pose my chile kain't help it?"

"She must help it. Tell her I say so."

"Oh, massa, ain't you gwine forgib my chile? She am mighty sorry she been an' gone an' done such a ting. She ain't neber gwine do de like ob dat no mo'."

"I trust not," he said; "I shall have to be very severe with her if she does. No, I am not ready to forgive her yet. Such conduct as she has been guilty of cannot be passed over with a trifling punishment. She must be made to realize that her offense is a very serious one."

A wave of his hand with the last word gave Chloe to understand that the interview was at an end.

Elsie's heart beat high betwixt hope and fear as she sat waiting and listening for Chloe's returning footsteps, and for her father's, which might perhaps accompany or precede them.

"Oh, mammy, what did he say? Will he forgive me? May I go to him now and call him papa?"

she asked, half breathlessly and with an eager, longing look as her nurse came in. Then, reading the answer in Chloe's sad and troubled countenance, she dropped her face into her hands and sobbed aloud.

"Don't chile; don't, honey darlin'. I'se sho it all come right befo' long," Chloe said tenderly, laying her hand caressingly on the drooping head. "But massa he say you mus' stop dis frettin' an' cryin'. I tole him s'pose you couldn't, but he say bery sternly, 'She must.' Kin you do it, darlin'?"

"I'll try. I must obey my father," she sighed. Lifting her head, she wiped away her tears, and by a strong and determined effort stopped their flow and suppressed her sobs.

It was now time for her preparations for bed. She went through them in silence, tears now and again gathering in her eyes, but none suffered to fall.

"Papa must be obeyed," she kept repeating to herself.

She maintained her self-control for some time after laying her head upon her pillow, but sleep did not visit it. As she lay there turning restlessly from side to side, mental distress again so overcame her that when she became aware of it, she was wetting her pillow with floods of tears and sobbing aloud.

It was now Mr. Dinsmore's own hour for retiring, and he was in his room, the door of communication with his little daughter's bedroom open as usual, so that the sound of her weeping came very distinctly to his ear.

The next moment, Elsie felt herself lifted from

the bed and set upon her feet, then her hand was taken in a close clasp, and she was led into the adjoining room, her own dressing room.

Here the moon shone brightly in at a window, in front of which stood an easy chair. Toward that her father led her, and seating himself therein, he was about to draw her to his knee. But she fell at his feet, sobbing, "Pa—oh, I can't help forgetting and calling you that, or crying because you are angry with me. But I don't want to be disobedient, and I'm so, so sorry for all my naughtiness. Please, please forgive me. Please let me call you father, or my heart will break!"

"You may. I remove the prohibition," he said in a moved tone, lifting her up and drawing her to his breast. "And if you are indeed very penitent on account of your very bad behavior yesterday, and promise never to do such a thing again, I will forgive and receive you back into favor."

"Dear father, thank you," she sobbed, clinging about his neck. "I think I was never so sorry in all my life, and I am quite resolved never, never to do such a thing again. I am astonished at myself to think I ever dared to do it."

"So am I," he said, "and I am afraid you are not fully sensible of the enormity of your offense. I want you to reflect that in that act, you were not only guilty of high-handed rebellion yourself but were encouraging and upholding your brother in the same. Do you wonder that I have felt it my painful duty to punish you with some severity?"

"No, papa," she answered humbly, "I feel that I have deserved it all, and a great deal more. I wonder you didn't whip me too, then and there, so that Horace might see how very naughty you considered my interference, and that I must obey just the same as he."

"I probably should have done just that had you been a little younger," he said, "and I am not altogether sure that I ought to have suffered you to escape as it was. You may be very sure," he added gravely and with some sternness of tone, "that you will not, if the offense is ever repeated."

"Oh, it shall not be, papa, it never, never shall!" she exclaimed, holding up her face for a kiss, which he gave heartily.

"To make sure of that, if you see such a conflict beginning (though I trust there will be no more of them), leave the room at once," he said.

They were silent for a moment, she with her head laid on his breast, her arm about his neck, while he held her close, softly smoothing the curls back from her brow with the free hand and gazing down tenderly into the little pale face with its tear-swollen eyes.

"My poor darling, you have had a sad time of it," he remarked presently. "You have been crying a great deal, I see."

At that, her face flushed painfully and her lip quivered. "Please, papa, don't be angry," she said in tremulous tones. "I tried to stop as soon as you sent me word and that I must. I didn't shed any more tears till after I got into bed, but then I was so, so hungry for my good-night kiss that they would come in spite of all I could do."

"Don't be afraid. I have forgiven all your offenses, and this is the seal," he said, kissing her fondly several times.

"Dear papa, thank you. Oh, how dearly I do love you! How sweet your caresses are to me!" she exclaimed. After a moment's silence, she asked, "Are mamma and Horace quite well, papa?"

"Yes. Both would have been in to to see you if their plans had met my approval. Horace was much concerned when I explained to him that because his sister was so very naughty as to try to take him away from me when I was punishing him for being stubborn and disobedient, she had to be punished too, and for that reason he could not see her."

"I am very much ashamed of having set him so bad an example, papa," she said with a sob, blushing deeply.

"It was to neutralize that example, not to mortify you, that I deemed it necessary to tell him. Now, my love, my darling, it is high time you were in bed and asleep," he added, repeating his caresses. Then, setting her on her feet again, he led her back to her bed, laid her in it, and with a fatherly blessing and a kiss on lip and cheek and forehead, left her to her slumbers.

At first she seemed too full of joy and thankfulness to close an eye, yet before she was aware of it, the happy waking thoughts had merged themselves in blissful dreams.

CHAPTER ELEVENTH

CROSSING THE PLAINS

NEWS WAS SEVERAL times received from Rupert and Don during their slow and toilsome journey across the states of Illinois and Missouri, but when the last frontier town was left behind—and with it such luxuries of civilization as mails and post offices—the door of communication was closed. They could neither hear from home nor be heard from there till the trackless wilderness should be crossed and the land of golden promise reached.

The Keiths had an ox team and wagon for the transportation of their baggage—clothing, camp equipage, mining tools, and some luxuries, among which were a few books. Also, a saddle horse, which they rode by turns, though Rupert oftener than Don, who had more strength for driving and more taste for it.

This emigrant band, of which they formed a part, comprised some twenty men, several with wives and children. There were a dozen wagons drawn by oxen and two or three horses beside that which were the joint property of Rupert and Don.

Rupert's health had steadily improved from the time of leaving home so that the bulletins to the dear ones there had been sources of great joy, though joy mingled with grief at the thought of the months or perhaps years that must pass by before they could hope to see the beloved wanderers again.

Rupert, who was of a very kindly disposition, always on the lookout for opportunities to be of service to others, had already become a general favorite with his fellow travellers.

If a little child was crying with the weariness of confinement to the cramped quarters of the wagon, he would take it on his horse before him and give it the rest of a brisk canter in the open air and with an unobstructed view on all sides.

Older ones were frequently taken up behind him, and at other times he dismounted and joined them as they plodded along beside or behind the wagons, beguiling the tediousness of the way with story or song.

So slow was the movement of the oxen, so wearisome the constant sitting or lying in the jolting wagons, that a robust child would very often prefer walking during the greater part of the day. And even little girls were known to have walked hundreds of miles in making the trip across the plains.

But it was necessary to keep near the wagons because of danger from wild beasts and roving bands of Indians.

Rupert, and indeed every man in the party, was always armed and ready to repel an attack or to bring down game that came within shooting distance, thus adding a welcome variety to their bill of fare. There were wild geese and turkeys, prairie fowl, rabbits, squirrels, deer, bison, and bears, all to be had for the shooting.

After leaving Independence, they camped out every night, building a fire to cook their evening meal and keep off wild beasts, except when there was reason to fear that Indians were in the neighborhood. Then the fire was not kindled, as the smoke would be likely to reveal their vicinity to the lurking foe. Instead, sentinels were posted who kept vigilant watch while the others slept.

Occasionally in the daytime, when no game had come near, two or three of the men would mount their horses and gallop away over the prairie in search of it, finding it no very difficult task to overtake the slow-moving wagon train, even after a ride of several miles and an absence, it might be, of an hour or more.

One afternoon, after they had been many weeks passing through that great wilderness, so that they were now much nearer California than the homes they had left behind, they were crossing a seemingly boundless rolling prairie.

Their provisions were getting low, and fowl and larger game alike had kept out of shooting range all day.

"It's five o'clock," Rupert Keith said, looking at his watch and addressing a man named Morton, who was riding by his side, "and will soon be too late for a shot at anything. Suppose we dash off over those hills yonder and see if we can't scare up something?"

"Agreed," said Morton. Then he called to another horseman, "Halloo, Smith! Will you join Keith and me in a run over those hills in search of game?"

"That I will!" was the rejoinder, and away they galloped and were in a few moments lost to the view of the rest of their party, who continued moving onward in their accustomed leisurely fashion.

An hour or more had passed; the prairie still stretched away on every side; the distant hills to the southward, beyond which the horsemen had gone, were still in view; and the eyes of almost every one in the train were turned ever and anon in that direction, hoping for their return well laden with venison or wild fowl.

At length a shout was raised, "Here they come!" But that was followed instantly by the affrighted cry, "Indians! Indians!" for a party of the latter were in full chase.

Don was walking beside his team, two little girls quite near him. He caught them up and almost threw them into his wagon, telling them to lie down and keep quiet and still, then turned and pulled out a revolver.

Others had acted with equal quickness and were ready—some from their wagons, some from the ground—to fire upon the advancing foe.

There was a brief, sharp flight. The Indians were driven off, carrying their killed and wounded with them.

Then it was found that Rupert was missing, Smith badly wounded, one or two others slightly, while Don lay insensible and bleeding on the ground near his wagon.

They at first thought him dead, but he had only fainted from loss of blood, and they presently succeeded in bringing him to.

"Rupert? My brother—where is he?" he asked in the first moment of consciousness.

"Those brutes have done for him, Don," Morton answered with a tremble in his voice. "The shot that tumbled him from his horse was the first intimation we had that they were upon us."

Don groaned and hid his face.

"Don't take it so hard," said a pitying woman's voice. "He's gone to a better place; we all know that. Nobody could be with him a day and not see that he was a real Christian."

"That's so." "True enough, Mrs. Stone." "I only wish we were all as ready for heaven," responded one and another.

Then Morton suggested that they ought to be moving on, for the Indians might return in larger force. It would not do to encamp where they were, and night was coming on.

To this there was a general assent. Don was carefully and tenderly lifted into his wagon and gently laid down upon the softest bed that could be improvised for him. Then a volunteer driver from among the young men of the party took his seat and drove on, doing his best to make the motion easy to the sufferer. They were the last of the train but not far behind the wagon next in front of them.

In spite of all the care and kindness shown him, Don's bodily sufferings were acute, yet by no means equal to his mental distress, his sense of bereavement—a bereavement so sudden, so shocking—and anguish at the thought of the poignant grief of his parents when the dreadful news should reach their ears.

The emigrants pushed on for several hours before they ventured to stop and encamp. When at last they did, the cessation of motion gave some slight relief to poor Don, and the food brought him by the kind-hearted woman who had tried to comfort him with the assurance of this brother's readiness for death revived somewhat his failing strength. But it was a night of pain and grief, in which Don would have given much to be at home again, especially if he might have had Rupert there alive and well.

The night passed quietly. There was no new alarm, and early in the morning the emigrants pursued their way, pressing forward as rapidly as circumstances would permit and keeping a sharp lookout for Indians.

Before they started—indeed, as soon as he was awake—Morton came to ask how Don was and how he had passed the night.

Don answered briefly, then burst out, "Oh, Morton, are you quite sure that—that my brother was killed? May he not have been only stunned by the shot and the fall from his horse?"

Morton shook his head. "No, I looked back several times, and he never moved."

"Oh," groaned Don, "if only I were not helpless, I should go and search for him, for I do not feel at all sure that he is not still alive."

"Well, I think you may," said Morton, "for even supposing he was not killed by that first shot and the fall, the Indians would be sure to finish him when they went back, for they went off in that direction."

Don turned away his face with a heavy sob. It

did indeed seem almost impossible that Rupert could have escaped death, and yet — and yet — oh, if he were but able to go in search of him! Perhaps he was a captive doomed to death by slow torture. Oh, to fly to his aid! To rescue or perish with him!

But no one else in all the company thought there was the least chance that he was alive, and to go in quest of him would not only greatly delay them (a great misfortune, considering the fact that their stock of provisions was so low) but would risk all their lives, as the Indians were probably still prowling about that spot and might attack them in great force.

The poor boy's only comfort was that, wherever and in whatever circumstances his brother might be, he was under the care of an almighty Friend who would never leave nor forsake him, and in being able to plead for him with that Friend.

The rest of the journey was, of course, a very sad one to poor Don, though everyone was kind to him, doing all that was possible for his relief and comfort, partly for Rupert's sake, partly for Don's own, for he too had ever shown a pleasant, obliging, kindly disposition toward others.

His wounds had nearly healed, and he had recovered almost his usual strength by the time their destination was reached.

Arrived there, he wrote at once to his parents, telling of Rupert's loss, his own condition, and asking if they were willing that, being now upon the ground, he should stay for a time and look for gold.

But as months must elapse before he could hope to receive an answer, he set to work and was determined to do his best in the meantime.

He did not find the life a whit less toilsome and trying than his parents had warned him it would be, nor were his surroundings any more agreeable. The roughest of men, drinking, smoking, swearing, quarrelsome creatures, were often his daily companions; the foulest language assailed his ears; gambling and drunken brawls went on in his presence; robberies, murders, and lynchings were of frequent occurrence; the Sabbath was openly desecrated; and men—even those who had been all their previous lives accustomed to the restraints of religion—here acted as if they had never heard of God, or heaven, or hell.

And there were few creature comforts to be had. All the necessaries of life were sold at astonishingly high prices, so that gold, even when found, could not be kept but instead melted away like snow in the sun.

It was not long before Don's thoughts were turned yearningly toward the home he had been so eager to forsake.

He was tolerably fortunate in his quest, but alas, all the gold in the world could not compensate for the loss of all the sweetness and beauty of life. All the happiness to be found in a well-regulated home, where love to God and man was the ruling principle of action; where were neatness and order, gentleness and refinement; where sweet-toned voices spoke kindly affectionate words; and affectionate smiles were wont to greet his coming, and loved eyes to look lovingly into his.

CHAPTER TWELFTH

There is that speaketh like the piercings of a sword.

—PROVERBS 12:18

MANY MONTHS HAD passed, bringing no news from their Westward-bound sons, and in spite of their trust in God, Mr. and Mrs. Keith were often not a little anxious.

Miss Stanhope had returned to her home in the fall after the boys' departure. Her pleasant, cheery companionship was much missed, and but for Mildred and Zillah being so near, the mother would have seen many a lonely hour, though she found agreeable occupation for a part of each day in teaching Annis, keeping her from school, and constituting herself her governess.

This took up the morning hours, while the married daughters were engaged with household cares and duties. Then the afternoons, if the weather permitted any of them to go from home, were usually spent together at one or another of the three houses, the ladies busy with their needles, the children playing about the room.

Both Mildred's and Zillah's cares were increasing, for each had now a little daughter. That made four little ones to claim the love of the grandparents and help to win their thoughts from the anxious following of the absent sons, and in that way they were proving great comforts as well as cares.

So the winter slipped quietly away without any startling event to mark its progress.

But in March Mrs. Keith had an attack of pneumonia, which greatly alarmed the family and kept her in bed for a fortnight. She was about again but still feeble and, in consequence of her weakness of body, more than ever anxious and distressed about Rupert and Don, from whom no news had yet been received since the letter from Independence so many, many months ago.

Mildred spent every spare moment with her mother, doing all in her power for her comfort of body and to cheer and interest her and keep her mind from dwelling upon the absent dear ones.

Dr. Landreth, too, was exceedingly kind to his mother-in-law, for whom he had a very strong and filial affection. He would have sacrificed his own comfort at any time for hers and was more than willing to have Mildred constantly with her while she was so feeble and ailing, while all his skill and medical knowledge were exerted for her benefit.

One evening while helping her mother to bed, Mildred remarked, "I wonder what has become of Charlie? He hasn't been in to see you this afternoon."

"Perhaps that is an evidence that he thinks me a great deal better," Mrs. Keith answered in a playful tone. Then, more seriously, "He has been very, very good to me, Mildred. You must tell him I appreciate his kindness."

"He knows you do, mother," Mildred answered."But indeed it is a real pleasure to him to do anything in his power for you. He says you are the only mother he has ever known, and a very dear and precious one."

"No doubt he would have been in this afternoon if he had not been prevented. I fear somebody is very ill."

A few minutes later Mildred, passing out of the house on her way to her own home, met her husband at the gate.

He gave her his arm almost without a voice, nor did he speak during their short walk. But Mildred's thoughts were busy, and she scarcely noticed his silence.

It was too dark in the street to see his face, but on entering their own sitting room, where a bright light was burning, she caught sight of it, and its pale, distressed look struck terror into her heart.

"Oh, Charlie, what is it?" she cried, dropping her cloak upon the floor and throwing off her bonnet, then putting her arms about his neck and gazing with frightened, questioning eyes into his that were full of anguish.

"My darling, I don"t know how to tell you," he said hoarsely, holding her close.

"My brothers?" she grasped, turning pale as death.

He bowed a silent assent.

"What—what is it?" she asked, scarcely able to articulate.

"The worst," he said. "It may not be true, but there is a dreadful report about town that the train was attacked by Indians and several killed—"

"Rupert and Don among them?" she faltered, half-inquiringly, as he paused, leaving his sentence unfinished.

"Yes. But, Milly dear, it may be altogether untrue."

She was clinging to him and weeping as if her very heart would break, her whole frame shaking with sobs.

"My brothers, my brothers! My dear, dear brothers!" she cried. "Oh, Charlie, Charlie, why did they ever go into such fearful danger?"

"I thought it for the best, love, when I advised it," he said in a pined tone. "But if I could have foreseen —"

"Dear husband, I forgot it was by your advice," she sobbed. "Forgive me. I should never think of blaming you."

"Thank you, love, I can hardly help blaming myself, though reason tells me I am innocent. Ah, if I could but have foreseen —"

"But you could not; no mortal could. Both killed? Both gone? Oh, it is too, too terrible!"

The door flew open and Zillah rushed in, closely followed by Wallace.

He was deathly pale, and his eyes were full of tears. She was weeping aloud.

"Oh, Milly, Milly!" she cried, "was there ever anything so terrible? It will kill mother. She can never stand it in her weak state."

"We must manage to keep it from her," the doctor said.

"How can we? She will see it in our faces," sobbed Zillah.

"We must control our features. And we must

banish every expression of grief from them and from our words and voices when in her presence. Her life may depend upon it, for she is very feeble just now."

"We will all try," Wallace said with a heavy sigh. "Let none of us venture into her presence until we are sure of ourselves."

"It will be very difficult, but I believe God will give us strength," said Mildred, "if we ask it in faith. Oh, it is an awful, awful thing!" she cried, a fierce paroxysm of grief sweeping over her. Then, growing calmer, she said, "But we have strong consolation in the certain knowledge that they were of those who trust in the imputed righteousness of Christ, that they had made their peace with God and were ready for the summons home."

"Yes," said Wallace, "we sorrow not as those without hope. And dear mother, who lives so near the Master and realizes so fully the blessedness of those who have gone to be forever with Him, will, I doubt not, be able to bear up under this new trial, terrible as it is, when she has regained her usual health."

"No doubt of it," the doctor said.

"But oh, it is so terrible, so terrible!" sobbed Zillah. "Far worse than any of the many trials that have come to us in the last two or three years."

"Does father know?" asked Mildred. "Has he heard?"

Neither the doctor nor Wallace could answer the question, for they had not seen him since early in the day.

But while they were saying so, the doorbell rang and he came in, bent, bowed down, aged with grief, till he looked an older man by ten—twenty—years than when they had seen him last.

With a moan of unspeakable anguish, he dropped into a chair and bowed his head upon his hands.

His daughters flew to him and enfolded him in loving arms, tears of sympathy streaming down their cheeks.

"Father, dear, dear father," they said, "oh, do not be so distressed! It may not be true."

"Alas, alas! I dare not hope it," he groaned. "My boys—my boys! Would God I had died for you! My sons, oh, my sons! Such a fate! Such a terrible fate!"

"But, dear father, think how happy they are now," said Mildred, weeping as she spoke.

"Yes, there is great and undeserved mercy mingled with the terrible affliction," he replied. "'They cannot return to me, but I shall go to them.' Thanks be unto God for that blessed hope! But my wife—your mother! This will kill her!"

"Dear father," said Mildred, "do not forget the precious promise, 'As thy days, so shall thy strength be.'"

"We have all agreed to try to hide it from her till she is stronger," the doctor remarked. "We will have to school ourselves to look and act and speak as if no such news had reached our ears."

"An impossible task, I fear," sighed Mr. Keith. "Marcia and I have had no secrets from each other since we were married, and it will be no easy task for me to conceal my anguish of heart from her now. But, God helping me, I will."

To father and daughters the next few days were

a severe ordeal, for it was difficult indeed to hide their bitter grief from the love-sharpened eyes of the tender wife and mother. They were cheerful when they could force themselves to be so, and when tears would have their way, they talked of Fan and seemed to be mourning afresh over her early death, or spoke of Ada in her far-distant home, and how faint was the hope that she would ever be with them again.

Mrs. Keith seemed somewhat surprised at these renewed manifestations of grief that had appeared to be softened by the lapse of time. But asking no questions, she simply talked to them of Fan's blessedness and the good work Ada was doing for the Master, and of the time when they would again be a united family in the glorious land where partings are unknown.

She was regaining strength every day, and in seeing that, they felt well regarded for their efforts at self-control and were encouraged to persevere with them. And they did, though at times—especially when she would speak of Rupert and Don, talking hopefully of soon hearing of their safe arrival in California—it was almost beyond their power, and they were compelled to find some pretext for leaving the room so that for a short space they might let grief have its way.

Mildred was sitting with her mother one morning, her babe asleep by her side in the cradle that had been occupied successively by herself and all of her brothers and sisters, Percy quietly busied with a picture book.

The two ladies had their sewing, and Annis was studying her lessons on the far side of the room.

The door bell rang, and Celestia Ann ushered in a woman, a resident of the town with whom the ladies had never had any acquaintance, though they knew her by name. Her call was therefore a surprise, but they gave her a pleasant "good morning" and a polite invitation to be seated.

She sat down, made a few remarks about the weather and the state of the roads, then, looking Mrs Keith full in the face, said, "I s'pose you've heard the news about the last party that set off from here for Californy?"

Mildred made a warning gesture, but it was too late and doubtless would not have been heeded even could it have been given in time.

"What news?" Mrs. Keith asked in a startled tone while Annis rose and came forward in an excited manner, her eyes wild with affright.

"So you haven't heard?" pursued the caller with the satisfaction of the newsmonger in a fresh customer for her wares. "Well—"

"Mrs. Slate," interrupted Mildred, "I must beg you to say no more. We have heard a vague report, which may be entirely untrue, but have been trying to keep it from mother, for she is too weak to bear it."

"What is it, Mildred, my child, what is it?" gasped the poor invalid, turning deathly pale.

"Dear mother, don't ask. It would only distress you, and it may be all a lie," Mildred said, going to her and putting her arms about her in tender, loving fashion.

"Tell me, my child. It is useless to try to keep me in ignorance now. Suspense would be worse than the direst certainty," faltered the mother.

"But there is no certainty, mother dear," Mildred said pityingly, her tears falling fast as she spoke. "Oh, be content not to hear what can but give you pain!"

"She'd ought to know," said Mrs. Slate. "She's got to hear it sooner or later, and what's the use of puttin' her off so? I'll tell you, Mrs. Keith. They say the train was attacked by the Indians, and most o' the men killed, your two boys among the rest. I felt it my duty to come and tell you about it, in case you hadn't heard, and to call your attention to the fact that this appears to be the way Providence has taken for to punish you for bringin' 'em up to care so much for gold, and—"

"Leave the house this instant, and never venture to darken its doors again!" cried Mildred, supporting her fainting mother with one arm while she turned, full of righteous indignation, toward her tormentor with a stamp of her foot to enforce the order she could not refrain from giving.

"I've only done my dooty," muttered the woman, rising and sailing from the room with her head in the air.

"Oh, mother, mother!" sobbed Mildred. "Annis, help me to lay her on the lounge and then run for Charlie. I think he's at home in the office. The cruel, cruel creature! How could she! Oh, *how could she!*"

Annis, wildly weeping, hastened to obey. "Oh, Milly, Milly, is mother dying? Is it true about the boys?"

"She has only fainted, and it is only a report about the boys that may not be at all true," Mildred said. "Now call Celestia Ann to help me, and you run for Charlie as fast as you can. Oh, Zillah,"she said in a tone of relief as the door opened and Mrs. Ormsby came in. "I'm glad you've come. Run to mother's room and get the bottle of ammonia."

Greatly startled and alarmed by the glimpse she had got of her mother's white, unconscious face, Zillah ran to do her sister's bidding, while Celestia Ann, summoned by Annis, hastened to render all the assistance in her power, and poor, terrified Annis flew like the wind in search of the doctor.

She found him in, and, though scarcely able to articulate, made him understand that his presence was wanted with all speed.

She darted back, and he caught up his medicine case and followed close at her heels.

Mrs. Keith still lay white and insensible, the three women busy about her with half-despairing efforts to restore her to consciousness.

They began to fear it was something more than an ordinary faint. Had that sudden, cruel announcement taken her life? Happy for her were it so, but oh, how could husband and children spare her?

Mildred turned upon her husband a look of agonized inquiry.

"Do not be alarmed, love," he said. "She will revive presently, I trust."

Some moments of trying suspense ensued, then her eyes opened wide and glanced about from one to another.

"What has happened?" she asked in feeble accents. "Have I been worse?"

"In a faint, mother. But you have come out of it now and, I hope, will be none the worse after a little," the doctor answered cheerfully. But as soon as the words had left his lips, memory had resumed her sway.

"Oh, my sons!" she cried. "My Rupert and Don! Can it be true that I shall see them no more upon earth? Have they been cut off in the pride and beauty of their early manhood by a deadly foe? O Lord, lead me to the Rock that is higher than I, for my heart is overwhelmed!" she cried, clasping her hands and lifting her streaming eyes to heaven.

"Dear mother," sobbed Mildred, leaning over her in tenderest solicitude. "If they are gone from earth, it is to the better land, where pain and sin and sorrow are unknown, and where you will one day join them and all your loved ones. But it may not be true! It is but a rumor."

"Then how cruel to tell me," she sighed, "and to add that I was to blame for their going. Ah, God knows I have tried to train them for heaven and not to set their affections upon the perishing things of time and sense."

"Yes, mother, your children can all testify to that," Mildred said. Zillah added, "Indeed we can! If any of us are worldly minded, it is not the fault of either of our parents. And it was not the love of gold that sent our dear brothers on that journey. One was seeking health; the other went to take care of him and with a longing for change and exciting adventure."

At that moment, Mr. Keith came in with a letter in his hand. His face was brighter and happier than they had seen it for many days, eagerness and anxiety mingling with its gladness.

"From Don to you, my dear," he cried, holding the letter high, with its address toward her.

"Oh, then it is not true! Not true!" was the simultaneous, joyful exclamation from his daughters. And Mildred, embracing the weeping invalid, said, "Do you hear that, dearest mother? A letter from Don, and you may dry your tears!"

Her husband held it out to her with a glad and loving smile.

She grasped it eagerly, but in vain her trembling fingers essayed to tear it open.

"Let me, dear wife," he said, taking it gently from her.

"Read it," she said feebly, "my eyes are dim. Oh, my Rupert! Is he living also?"

Mr. Keith glanced down the page, let the letter fall, and dropped his face into his hands with a heart-rending groan.

Zillah snatched it from the floor, her hand trembling like an aspen leaf, her face overspread with a deathly pallor.

"My son, my son, my first-born son!" sobbed Mrs. Keith, "Gone, gone in that dreadful way! Yet, thank God that dear Don is left. And blessed be His holy name that He lives and reigns, and none can stay His hand or say unto Him, 'What doest thou?'"

"Read, someone," groaned the father; "I cannot!"

Zillah silently handed the letter to the doctor, and he read it in low, moved tones, often interrupted by the bitter weeping of his listeners.

Rupert's death was a heavy blow, and for a time his parents seemed well nigh crushed by it, yet not a murmur was ever heard fro either. The language of their lips and lives was, "'Though He slay me, yet will I trust in Him.'"

The manner of their son's death made it the hardest blow they had ever received, yet as the months rolled on, they learned to speak calmly and tenderly of him as having gone before to the heavenly home where they themselves would soon follow.

Don's letter received a reply in due time. It said his speedy return would be joyfully welcomed, yet as he was now on the ground, he was free to stay for a time if such were his choice. So he remained, fascinated by the hope of success in his search for gold and feeling a great repugnance to going back and facing his townsmen without having secured a least a moderate portion of that which he had come so far to find.

CHAPTER THIRTEENTH

No day discolored with domestic strife;
No jealousy, but mutual truth believ'd,
Secure repose, and kindness undeceived.

— DRYDEN

MONTHS AND YEARS glided swiftly by, bringing to the Keiths only such changes as they will bring to all: added gray hair and wrinkles and a decrease of strength, vigor, and energy to the old people; to the younger married ones, an added staidness and dignity of demeanor and more olive branches about their tables; while Annis had grown from the merry, romping child into a tall, slender maiden, even more comely than the child had been but with a quieter step and often a dreamy, faraway look in the sweet blue eyes.

She was the joy of her parents' hearts, the very light of their eyes, the only child left at home, for Cyril, having completed his college course, had entered a theological seminary and was preparing to go into the ministry.

There had been all along a constant interchange of letters with their relatives at the Oaks, particularly brisk on the part of Annis and Elsie, and they each knew almost as much of the thoughts, feelings, and experiences of the other as though they had lived together all these years.

Letters from the Oaks were always joyfully welcomed yet were esteemed as nothing in comparison with those that came occasionally from Ada and Don, the former of whom had become the happy mother of two children, whom she described as very sweet and lovable, adding that she had a great longing to show them to her father and mother. And it was perhaps not greater than the desire of the grandparents to see them, though that was far outweighed by their thirst for a sight of the mother's face.

Mildred was still the devoted daughter she had been in earlier days, nor was she less faithful in all that concerned the welfare of husband and children. She looked well to the ways of her household, and never ate the bread of idleness. She was a careful housekeeper, allowing no waste, yet she was most liberal in paying for every service done for her or hers, and was never stinting in the provision for the wants of her family.

Her table was always bountifully provided, her house neat and clean, her children well and tastefully dressed, her husband's wardrobe carefully looked to. Nor did she neglect the souls, minds, or bodies of her children. Their physical wellbeing was to her a matter of very great importance, and while assiduously cultivating their minds and hearts, letting them never want for mother love and tender caresses, she watched over the health of each with untiring vigilance.

And she had her reward in their rosy cheeks,

bounding steps, constant flow of animal spirits, and devoted love to their parents, especially their mother, and also in their kindness and affection toward each other.

They were a very happy family, a joy of heart to Mr. and Mrs. Keith, as were Zillah's children also, she having greatly improved in her management as a mother since the babyhood of her first child.

It was springtime again, the evenings still cool enough for a little fire to be very enjoyable. In Dr. Landreth's cozy sitting room a bright wood fire blazed cheerily on the open hearth. The doctor himself sat over it alone and in meditative mood.

Mildred had left the room a moment before to see her children to bed, a duty she never neglected, and not only a duty but a pleasure also, for it gave opportunity for many a sweet interchange of demonstrations of affection and many a childish confidence to mother which otherwise might have been withheld. Also—the young hearts being warm, the feelings tender—she found it the best of all seasons for sowing good seed that might one day spring up and grow and bear fruit unto everlasting life.

The doctor's meditations seemed not unpleasant, if one might judge from the calm and placid expression of his countenance. Yet occasionally there was a passing shade of doubt or anxiety.

He looked up with a smile as Mildred reentered the room. "Come and sit by my side, wife," he said, "and let us have a confidential chat. Do you know what I have been thinking, sitting here alone?" he asked as she took the offered seat and his arm stole round her waist in very lover-like fashion.

"No, my dear, how should I?" she answered with a smile. "Of your patients, I presume. Some case of obscure and difficult diagnosis."

"Ah, you are wide of the mark," he returned with a light laugh. "No, my thoughts were principally of the presiding genius of my happiest of homes, and I am ready to echo the words of the wise man, 'A prudent wife is from the Lord.' 'Whoso findeth a wife, findeth a good thing and obtaineth favor of the Lord.'"

"You're satisfied with yours?" she said inquiringly and with a glad look up into his face.

"More than satisfied! Milly, love, you are my greatest earthly treasure, dearer far to me now than the day we were married, though then I was sure I loved you as never man loved woman before."

"How you gladden my heart, my dearest and kindest of husbands," she said in low, moved tones. "And my experience is the same as yours. I loved you dearly when we were married, but I love you ten times as dearly now. How sweet it is to live together as we do, with hearts so closely united and ever sharing each other's joys and sorrows! Burdens thus divided are so much easier to bear, while joys are doubled in the sharing."

"Yes, it is so," he said.

> "'Then come the wild weather—come sleet or come snow,
> We will stand by each other, however it blow;
> Oppression and sickness, and sorrow and pain,
> Shall be to our true love as links to the chain.'"

They talked about their children, now three in number, and of their various dispositions, and the best mode of managing and training each.

After that, breaking a pause in the conversation, the doctor said, "By the way, Milly, I received a letter today from a second cousin of mine, telling me that a daughter of hers, a young lady, is in poor health, needing change of climate and scene, her physician says, and asking if I am willing to take her under my care for a time, probably until next fall. My love, would you like to take her into the family?"

"I am quite willing if it is your wish, my dear," Mildred answered but with a slight sigh. They were so happy and peaceful by themselves, and this stranger might prove an element of discord.

"It is not my wish if at all unpleasant to you, wife," he said with affectionate look and tone. "I fear it may add to your cares and labors, yet Flora Weston may prove one of those bright, merry, winsome young things that are like a fresh breeze in a house."

"Perhaps so. And we are told to use hospitality one to another without grudging," Mildred added with a pleasant look and smile. "Write her at once, Charlie, if you feel inclined. I am glad of an opportunity to show some attention to a relative of yours."

"Just like you, Milly," he responded with a gratified look.

The letter was sent the next day, and a few weeks later Miss Weston arrived.

She seemed a rather commonplace girl, quiet and undemonstrative. Mildred found it a task to entertain her, even with the assistance her mother and sisters could give, and they did all that lay in their power. She did not sew, she cared very little for reading, she had strength for only short walks, she was no talker, and she seldom seemed to care to listen.

Annis soon voted her an intolerable bore, yet, to relieve Milly, she spent several hours of every day in her society. The doctor did his share by taking her with him whenever he drove into the country. He made many attempts to draw her out, both then and when he had an evening at home, but not succeeding, he finally came to the conclusion that there was nothing in her.

He would have wholly regretted having invited her but that her health presently began to improve under his treatment.

Meanwhile, Flora was silently observing all that went on in the family, especially studying Mildred, and at length her manner—which had at first been very cold and distant—gradually changed till there was at times a warmth of affection to it.

"You are so kind to me, Cousin Mildred," she said one day. "You have never neglected anything that could add to my comfort and have always shown so much sympathy for my invalidism, far more than ever my own mother did," she added in a bitter tone. "Mother is very good and pious, but she has never taken any care of her children's health. She is duly anxious about our souls but neglects our bodies. I must acknowledge that I came here strongly prejudiced against you, simply because I had heard you were very pious, and the way I have been brought up had made me hate piety, hate the Bible and prayer."

"Oh, Flora! And you the child of a Christian mother!" cried Mildred in a shocked tone.

"Yes, I believe mother is a real Christian, and I don't wonder you are shocked at what I have said. But if she had brought me up as you do your children, I am sure I should have felt quite differently. Is it any wonder I hate the Bible when, instead of being entertained when good with beautiful stories out of it, I was always punished when particularly naughty by being forced to read a certain number of chapters in proportion to the extent of my delinquency and to commit so many verses to memory, besides being prayed over—a long tedious prayer, half of which I did not understand?"

"I have always tried to make the Bible a delight to my children," said Mildred, "and I think it is. Oh, Flora, I feel very sorry for you that you do not appreciate its beauty and sweetness! Are you not old enough now to put away your unfortunate prejudice and learn to love it as God's own word given to teach us how to obtain eternal life—telling the old, old story, the sweet, sweet story of Jesus and His love?"

"I have begun to like it better since I came here," Flora answered with an abashed look. "I have really enjoyed the Bible stories I have overheard you telling the children, and somehow religion seems a lovelier thing as I see it exhibited in your life and the lives of Cousin Charlie and your parents and sisters than as my mother practices it."

"It grieves me to hear a daughter speak so of her mother," Mildred said gently.

"I don't mean to be unkind or disrespectful toward her," replied Flora, "but I wish to make you understand how I came to feel such a prejudice against piety, and against you because I had been told you were very pious.

"I am quite sure mother is good and sincere and not at all puffed up and self-righteous, but I think she makes great mistakes which prejudice people against her religion.

"Now, my father is not a pious man, and some things mother does, and her refusal to do some other things, have so turned him against religion that he never goes inside of a church door.

"For one thing, mother won't dress like other ladies. He wants to see her well dressed, but she makes it a part of her religion to go looking old-fashioned and really dowdy. Father buys her handsome things, and she won't wear them. She gives them away or cuts them up for the children, and I don't wonder that he won't go to church with her. I am pretty sure he might have become a regular attendant if she would only have dressed to suit him.

"And sometimes she gets out of her warm bed, on a cold winter night, and goes off into a room where there is no fire and stays there for an hour or more—in her bare feet and her nightdress—praying. Then she comes back chilled through, probably has a dreadful cold the next day, and that makes father mad, and he lays it all to her religion.

"I love my mother, Cousin Mildred, but I can't help blaming her for at least part of my sufferings. As I have told you, she has never taken care of her children's health. If our food was improperly cooked, it was a matter of no importance, and just so if our clothing, beds, or bedding were left unaired or if any other sanitary measure were disregarded. We were often forced to eat and sleep in a close, almost stifling atmosphere. We wore our winter clothes into the heat of summer and our thin summer clothing far on into the damp, cold days of autumn and early winter.

"Then, too, when I began to complain of this dreadful pain in my back, no notice was taken, and I was expected to do as much as if I were perfectly well and strong. She would not hire as much help as she might, as father was quite willing she should, and I was often left to do everything while she spent hours at a time in her closet.

"I've thought sometimes that life would have been easier for me if I'd had a worldly minded mother who would have taken some care of my health. And I expected to find you the same kind of Christian, but you are very different."

"I fear the difference is not all in my favor," Mildred said.

"But don't you think health ought to be taken care of?" asked Flora. "I have noticed that you are very careful of your children's, as well as of their morals and manners."

"Yes," Mildred said, "I think the Bible teaches very plainly that we are to be careful of our bodies. 'What? know ye not that your body is the temple of the Holy Ghost which is in you, which ye have of God, and ye are not your own?' Health is one of God's good gifts and not to be despised; it is one of the greatest of temporal blessings. Besides, to be careless of it is to lessen our ability to work for God and probably to shorten our lives, which we certainly have no right to do.

"But, Flora, perhaps I am not so different from your mother as you think. I, too, love to spend an hour alone in communion with my best Friend, and I do not find it time lost, for thus I gather strength for the duties, trials, and temptations of life. I never could meet them without the strength and wisdom that He gives in answer to prayer."

"But you don't seem to neglect other duties for that," Flora said with an earnest, inquiring look at Mildred.

"I hope not," was the answer. "The Bible tells us there is a time for everything, and it bids us 'be diligent in business' but also 'fervent in spirit, serving the Lord.' It tells us, 'In everything give thanks,' and also bids us 'pray without ceasing,' so that it is evident that we need not always retire into the closet to talk with our heavenly Father, but that while our hands are busy with the work He has given us to do, we may, and should be, ever and anon lifting up our hearts in silent prayer to Him.

"Oh, Flora, what a blessed privilege it is to be permitted to do that at all times and in all places! When in doubt, to ask Him for wisdom and guidance, though it be in regard to but a seemingly trivial matter (for great events often hang upon trifles). When tempted to indolence, petulance, censoriousness, or any other sin, to be able on the instant to send up a cry for strength to resist, a cry to Him who is the hearer and answerer of prayer and who has all power in heaven and in earth. Or if danger threatens one's self or one's dear ones, what a relief to be able to call at once for help to One who is mighty to save!"

Flora was in a, for her, surprisingly talkative mood. "Cousin Mildred," she said, "I have been admiring the good behavior of your children ever since I came here. They are so obedient, so gentle-mannered, and so polite to you and their father, to each other, and indeed to everybody. How have you managed to make them so?"

"There is no great secret about it," Mildred said, smiling. "We try to teach them politeness and consideration for others by both precept and example. My husband is always quite as polite and attentive to me as he could be to any strange lady guest. I try to be the same to him, and we both treat our children in the same manner. We never give a command when a request will answer as well, and we seldom meet with any hesitation in obedience. But if we do, I assure you we resort to command and enforce it, too."

"Do you teach them they must obey because you are their parents?" asked Flora with a look of keen curiosity.

"Certainly we do," Mildred answered in some surprise.

"I once read a description of a very nice kind of mother," explained Flora—"at least the author evidently meant her for a model—and one thing he said in her praise was that she never claimed a right to her child's obedience on the plea that she was his mother."

"Then," said Mildred gravely, "he was either unacquainted with the teachings of God's Word or had no respect for them, for there are very many passages that teach children the duty of obedience to parents, and others that command parents to see to it that their children are obedient to them.

"There is the fifth commandment, 'Honor thy father and thy mother: that thy days may be long upon the land which the Lord thy God giveth thee.' Again, 'Children, obey your parents in the Lord: for this is right.' 'Honor thy father and mother; which is the first commandment with promise.' 'My son, keep thy father's commandment, and forsake not the law of thy mother,' and many others.

"Then to parents, 'Correct thy son, and he shall give thee rest; yea, he shall give delight unto thy soul,' and many others of like import, while Solomon tells us, 'A child left to himself bringeth his mother to shame.'

"And how sorely Eli was punished for not restraining his sons when they made themselves vile. Also, God says, in commendation of Abraham, 'I know him, that he will command his children and his household after him, and they shall keep the way of the Lord to do justice and judgment.' And do you not remember that under the Levitical law, the punishment of a refusal to be obedient to parents was death?"

"Is that so? I had quite forgotten it," said Flora.

Mildred opened a Bible, and turning to the twenty-first chapter of Deuteronomy, read aloud, "'If a man have a stubborn and rebellious son, which will not obey the voice of his father, or the voice of his mother, and that, when they have chastened him, will not hearken unto them: then shall his father and his mother lay hold on him, and bring him out unto the elders of his city, and unto the gate of his place; and they shall say unto the elders of his city, This our son is stubborn and rebellious, he will not obey our voice; he is a glutton, and a drunkard. And all the men of his city shall stone him with stones, that he die; so shalt thou put evil away from among you; and all Israel shall hear and fear.'"

"I acknowledge that you have proved your case against my author," said Flora thoughtfully. "Either he was ignorant of the teachings of Scripture on that point, or he chose to disregard them, which nobody has a right to do."

"No, that is true," said Mildred. "As the Word of God, whose creatures we are, it should be to all of us the rule of faith and practice, a tribunal from which there is no appeal, whose decisions are final."

"I have noticed," remarked Flora, "that you all seem to regard it in that light and to have a great love for it, too."

"Yes," said Mildred, "and no wonder. Its precious promises have been our comfort and support in many trials—some of them very heavy. I think those sweet promises were all that kept my mother's heart from breaking when she heard that her two sons had been killed by the Indians."

"It must have been dreadful," Flora said with sympathy, "but it wasn't true?"

Not of both, but of one," Mildred answered with emotion. "Oh, my dear, dear brother!" she cried, in a sudden burst of grief.

Flora went to her and put her arms about her. "Don't weep so," she said. "Think how happy he is where he has gone, and how safe. No one can ever make him suffer again."

"I know, and what a comfort it is!" said Mildred. "What joy in the thought that we shall all meet at last in that blessed land, never to part again and to be forever with the Lord!"

From that day Flora seemed a changed girl, ready to talk and to take an interest in those about her, to appreciate and respond to their efforts to entertain her, and she was particularly demonstrative and affectionate toward Mildred.

Chapter Fourteenth

The Return

Joy never feasts so high
As when the first course is of misery.

—Suckling

ON A PLEASANT October day the three families—including Miss Weston—were gathered at Mr. Keith's for a family tea party, no very unusual occurrence.

The railroad had recently reached Pleasant Plains, and a few minutes before the call to tea the whistle of the afternoon train from the West had been heard.

They had but just seated themselves about the table, and Mr. Keith had asked a blessing on the food, when the door opened and a stranger entered unannounced.

Everyone looked up in surprise as he stood silently gazing at the mother.

The next instant, she sprang up with a joyful cry and threw herself into his outstretched arms, weeping hysterically.

"Don!" was the simultaneous exclamation from the others, and they gathered about him laughing and crying together in their joyous excitement.

Yes, it was Don, and no other — Don who went away a smooth-faced boy and had come back a bearded man.

With what a rapture of delight they embraced and welcomed him, yet delight mingled with grief, for how could they forget that two had gone out from the, and but one had returned? Celestia Ann stood outside of the circle, leaning her back against the wall and gazing at Don, the big tears streaming down her homely but kindly face. At length, stepping forward, she caught his hand in a vise-like grasp, saying, "It's Mister Don, sure enough, though I wouldn't a knowed him by his looks. They've all been a-huggin' and kissin' of you, and now it's my turn," she said, catching him round the neck and giving him a resounding kiss. "You'll not mind, will you? Seein' as I've know'd ye ever since you was a little feller — a mere baby, as one may say."

"I am very glad to find you here still, Celestia Ann," Don said with a good-humored laugh. "And I don't object to the heartiness of your welcome, for I haven't had a kiss from a woman since I left home, until today."

"Well, no, I reckon not. I shouldn't never b'lieve you was the kind of a feller to be a-kissin' strange womenfolks. But now why on airth don't ye all set down and eat? Mr. Don must be awful hungry, a-comin' all the way from Californy here."

"Most assuredly, if he has had nothing to eat since he started," laughed the doctor, resuming his place at the table, with all the others doing likewise.

Then they remembered to introduce the returned wanderer to Flora, who had been a silent but not unmoved spectator of the little scene.

Far more talking than eating ensued.

Don did greater justice to the viands than most of the others, who were much occupied in looking at and listening to him, his mother especially. She feasted her eyes on his face and lost not a tone of the voice she had for years feared she might never hear again this side the grave.

And he was perforce the chief speaker, though he had many questions to ask of relatives, friends, and acquaintance.

Parents, sisters, and brothers-in-law wanted to know all he had seen, done, and suffered, and they plied him with questions till his mother remarked they were making him talk too much and giving him no chance to eat.

"And it is the very best meal I have sat down to since I went away nearly four years ago. I ought to be allowed to do it justice," laughed Don.

They were a long while at the table, yet Celestia Ann showed no impatience, though usually she was in great haste to "get the table cleared and the dishes washed up."

But at last they all withdrew to the parlor.

It was verging upon ten o'clock, yet no one seemed to have thought of bed, though Don might well have been supposed to be tired from his long and wearisome journey. Mildred and Zillah had taken their babies home, seen them safely to bed, and, leaving them in the care of their nurses, returned to the circle gathered in the parlor of their father's house.

Don was telling some of his adventures, and no one but Celestia Ann in the kitchen noticed the ringing of the door bell.

She, hastening to answer it, found a tall man, wearing a very heavy beard and mustache, standing there.

"Good evening," he said with a polite inclination of the head. "Is my—is Mrs. Keith in?"

Celestia Ann staggered back, turning very pale in the light of the lamp that hung suspended from the ceiling. "I—I should say I knowed that voice if—if the feller that owned it hadn't been killed dead by the Injuns more'n three years back; leastways so we heard tell," she gasped. "Be ye Rupert Keith, or his ghost?"

"I am no ghost, Celestia Ann," he said with a smile. "Reports are sometimes quite untrue, as was the one you speak of."

She grasped his hand and burst out sobbing for very joy.

"There, there!" he said kindly. "I am afraid mother will hear and be alarmed. If she should hurry out and find me here—so unexpectedly—it might be more than she could well bear."

"Yes, she'd ought to be prepared, 'specially as she's had one great surprise a'ready today in Don's comin'—"

"What! Is Don here? Just returned?" he cried. "Oh, but that is good news! They're in the parlor, I think. I'll go into the sitting room and get you to call Dr. Landreth out (the rest will suppose he's wanted to see a patient), and he can prepare my mother."

"A first-rate plan, Mr. Rupert," said Celestia

Ann. Waiting till he reached the door of the sitting room, she opened that of the parlor.

"Doctor," she said, "there's a man out here a-wantin' to speak to ye."

"Oh, I hope it isn't a call to the country," remarked Mildred, as her husband made haste to obey the summons.

The conversation in the parlor went on, no one supposing the caller a person in whom any of them had an interest.

As the doctor entered the sitting room the stranger rose and held out his hand. "Very glad to see you again, Dr. Landreth. You have not forgotten me?" he said inquiringly and with a humorous look.

"I am afraid I have, sir, if ever I had the pleasure of your acquaintance," was the reply as the offered hand was taken and the doctor gazed doubtfully into the bronzed and bearded face.

"Ah, Charlie, is your memory so short?" Rupert asked in a half-reproachful tone, holding fast his brother-in-law's hand and looking him steadily in the eyes.

"Why!" gasped the doctor, "It isn't—it can't be—"

"Yes, it can be, and it is," laughed Rupert, though his voice trembled with emotion. "God has mercifully spared me and brought me back again to my father's house. Are all well? Can you prepare my mother for the news that I am yet alive and here?"

"In a moment—when I have myself so far recovered from the shock as to be fully able to control my voice," answered the doctor jokingly but with a very perceptible tremble in his tones. "My dear fellow, if I am so overcome with happiness, what will she be?"

"Joy seldom kills?" Rupert said interrogatively.

"Rarely. And yet it has been fatal in some instances, so we must move with caution."

He stepped into the hall, opened the parlor door, and called softly to his wife.

She came to him at once. "What is it? Has baby wakened?"

He gently drew the door to behind her before he answered. Then, taking her in his arms, he said tenderly, "Milly, love," and she noticed that his voice was unsteady. "Can you bear very great joy?"

She gave him a startled look. "What is it? Oh, Rupert? No, no, that cannot be!"

"Yes, dearest, news has come that his—that the report of his death was false—"

"Is he here?" she gasped. "Oh, Charlie, don't keep me in suspense! Take me to him!"

"I did not say he was here, love, only that he was still alive at last reports."

But through the half-open door of the sitting room she had caught a glimpse of a tall form that wore a strangely familiar look. Breaking from her husband's arms, she ran to see who it was, and ran into the arms of her long-lost and deeply mourned brother, outstretched to receive her.

He held her close, she weeping hysterically on his breast. "Dear, dear brother! Where, where have you been so long—so very long!—while we wept and mourned for you as dead?"

"A captive among the Indians," he answered. "Tell me, has there been any break in the dear circle since I went away?"

"No, we are all here."

"Thank God for that!" he said with reverent gratitude. "And now I must see my mother. I can wait no longer."

"Just one moment. I will send father out and break the good news to her as gently and cautiously as I can," Mildred said, and she glided away through the hall and into the parlor, her eyes full of glad tears, her face radiant with joy.

"Someone in the sitting room wishes to see you, father," she whispered to him. Then, turning to the others as he rose and went out, she was opening her lips to speak when Annis exclaimed, "Why, Milly, you look as if you had found a gold mine!"

"Better than that," cried Mildred, dropping on her knees by her mother's side and putting her arms about her. "Mother, dear, can you bear the best of good tidings?"

"What is it, child? Tell me at once. Nothing is so hard to bear as suspense," said Mrs. Keith, turning pale. "Has Ada come home? Don't keep me from her a moment," she said, rising hastily, as if to hurry from the room.

"No, mother, not that, but still better and stranger news," Mildred said, gently forcing her back into her seat. "A gentleman just returned from the far West brings the news that our Rupert was only taken prisoner by the Indians, not killed."

Mrs. Keith seemed about to faint, a sudden, death-like pallor overspread her face, and Don threw his arm round her.

"Mother, dear, it is good news! What could better?" he said, his voice quivering with excitement and joy.

"Yes," she responded, her color coming back. "Oh, can it be possible that my son yet lives? 'Oh that men would praise the Lord for his goodness and for his wonderful works to the children of men!'"

Then, starting to her feet, she added, "Is the gentleman here? I must see him, speak to him, hear all he can tell me of my dear boy."

"Oh, wait just a moment, mother, dear," Mildred said, springing up and laying a detaining hand on her mother's arm. "Father has gone out to speak to him. Ah, here he is," she said as Mr. Keith reentered the room, his face shining with joy, every feature quivering with emotion.

He stepped hurriedly toward the little group. "Wife! Wife!" he cried, catching her in his arms. "Our boy, our dear Rupert! We have not lost him yet. He is restored to us as from the grave. He lives! He lives! Thank God for his unmerited goodness and mercy!"

Rupert had followed his father, and standing at the half-open parlor door, thence catching a glimpse of his mother's beloved face, he could restrain himself no longer.

In another moment he had her in his arms, holding her close and covering her face with kisses.

She did not faint but lay on his breast weeping for joy as if she would weep her very life away, the rest looking on and weeping with her.

At last she lifted her head for a long, searching gaze into his face, the dear face she had not thought ever to see again on earth. "You have changed," she said, the tears streaming down her cheeks. "You have grown older, darker — there are lines of care and suffering my heart aches to see — but it is my own boy still, and your mother's eyes would have recognized you anywhere."

"And you, dearest mother, have grown so thin and pale, your hair so white," he said with emotion.

"Never mind, my son, I shall grow young again now," she answered with a touch of her old-time merriment. Then, gently withdrawing herself from his arms, she looked on with eyes full of glad tears while brothers and sisters, each in turn, embraced and rejoiced over the lost and found again.

Perhaps the most affecting part of the scene was the meeting of the two brothers, each of whom had long believed the other slain.

But it was a moving spectacle throughout. Celestia Ann, peering in at the door, cried heartily from very sympathy, and Flora Weston, feeling like an intruder upon the sacred privacy of the family, stole quietly away to Dr. Landreth's, leaving word with Celestia Ann that she had gone, "thinking it time for an invalid to be in bed."

But it was long before her absence was noticed. Rupert did not attempt to tell his story that night; it was much too long, he said. Tomorrow he would gather them all about him, if they liked, and go in to the details. In the meanwhile, there is something which he must say at once.

"I shall greatly surprise you all, I know," he said with a happy smile. "Mother," he continued, turning to her, "do not be shocked when I tell you that I have brought a wife with me."

He read a look of astonishment, not unmixed with dismay, on every face, but they waited in silence to hear what more he had to say.

"She is a Mexican," he went on, "of Spanish descent, and very beautiful, I think. But better still, she is a Protestant. We were fellow captives, and I doubtless owe my life to her kind and skilful nursing."

"Then we will all welcome her!" exclaimed both his parents in a breath. "Where is she now?"

"At the hotel. She feared to come upon you without previous announcement. In fact, she is very much afraid of being unwelcome as it is," Rupert answered with a wistful glance from one to another of the beloved faces about him.

"Tell her she needn't," cried Mildred with impulsive warmth. "Say that we owe her a debt of gratitude it will be impossible ever to pay, if she is a good and loving wife to the dear brother whose life she has saved."

"Yes, tell her that," said his mother. "Go and bring her to us. She shall have a daughter's welcome from me."

"May I go with you?" Don asked as Rupert rose to go.

"And I?" added the father, rising also. "We will assure her of her welcome before she has to face us all here."

"I feel inclined to go myself," said the mother, smiling affectionately upon Rupert. "But no, on second thought, I should rather have our first interview here, with no prying eyes to look on."

"Yes, that will be best. But — " he said, glancing a little wistfully at his sisters.

All three at once offered to accompany him.

"Thank you, you dear girls," he said heartily, "but some of you should stay with mother."

After a little discussion it was agreed that Zillah should go, the others to await the coming of the new sister where they were.

The hotel was at no great distance, and they had not long to wait. The little party presently returned, and Rupert led proudly up to his mother one of the most beautiful, graceful, and altogether bewitching young creatures she had ever seen.

"Mother, this is your new daughter. Juanita, our mother," he said, and they embraced with warmth of affection.

"I love you now for my dear son's sake and all that he tells me you have done for him, and I hope very soon to love you for your own," Mrs. Keith said. "I, too, the same for my Rupert's sake," the girl wife answered in liquid tones and pure English, only a slight and pretty accent betraying the fact that it was not her native tongue. "I hope you will be my dearest mamma, if it so be that you can love a foreigner."

"We will not call or consider you that, dear child," responded Mrs. Keith with feeling, bestowing another kiss upon the rich red lips. "Rupert tells me you are a Christian, and 'we are all one in Christ Jesus,' no more strangers and foreigners but fellow citizens with the saints and of the household of God . . . Jesus Christ himself being the chief cornerstone."

"Oh, thanks, then we will love one another very much," said the young bride, tears of joy shining in her beautiful dark eyes. "Now I feel that I shall be very happy in my husband's dear home that he has told me of so many, many times."

"I hope you will," Mildred said, embracing her affectionately in her turn. "I trust we shall become dear sisters to each other. We all want you to feel at home among us."

Annis came next. "I am your youngest sister," she said, bestowing and receiving a kiss. "At least the youngest here."

"I have none other," returned the bride in slightly saddened tones. "My husband," and she turned a look of ineffable affection upon Rupert, "is all I have. Father, mother, brother, sister I have none."

"Ah, we must indeed be kind to you, poor lonely dear!" said Mrs. Keith.

But it was growing late, and the travellers were weary from the long journey.

Mr. Keith read a short psalm of praise, every heart echoing the words, and they sang the Doxology: "Praise God from whom all blessings flow." A short prayer of fervent thanksgiving followed, and they separated for the night, Annis full of delight at the thought of how deeply interested Elsie would be in the story she meant to write her of the strange and wonderful events of this day.

For very joy the parents could not sleep. They lay awake a long while talking of their sons and the new daughter.

"She looks very young," Mr. Keith remarked.

"About eighteen, I should think," said his wife. "Poor lonely dear! We must be very kind to her, especially for what she did for Rupert."

"As kind as we know how to be," said Mr. Keith. "I cannot yet quite overcome a feeling of repugnance at the thought of a foreigner as a daughter-in-law, but I trust I shall be able to in time. And in the meanwhile, I certainly intend to treat her as well as if I were delighted with the match."

"She is very beautiful," remarked his wife. "What lovely, expressive eyes she has!"

"Very, and they gaze at Rupert as if he were a sort of demigod in her opinion," laughed the father. A happy, gleeful laugh it was.

"Our boy's return is making you young again, Stuart," said his wife.

"Both of us, I hope, my dear," he responded. "But now we must try to sleep, or I fear we shall feel old in the morning."

The whole family were disposed to think well of the new member and make her quite one of themselves, especially for Rupert's sake. Don expressed himself as delighted with her looks and manners, and "How beautiful she is!" "Yes, perfectly lovely," were the sentences exchanged between Mildred and Zillah as they left their father's door that night to go to their own homes. And Flora received quite an enthusiastic description of her charms from the doctor when they met at the breakfast table the next morning.

"Did you see our new sister last night, Celestia Ann?" asked Annis, busy adorning the breakfast table in her home with flowers.

"Yes, I reckon I did, Annis. Wasn't I in to the readin', prayin', and singin'? Yes, I seen her, and I think she's about the purtiest creeter that I ever sot eyes on. I on'y hope she'll turn out as good as she's purty. I wisht she wasn't a furriner, though, for somehow I can't seem to like 'em quite so well as our own folks."

Chapter Fifteenth

Calamity is man's true touchstone.

IN THEIR RETREAT after the attack upon the emigrant train to which Rupert and Don belonged, the Indians passed again over the ground where they had shot down the former.

He still lay motionless and insensible, just as he had fallen from his horse. Several of the savages dismounted and stooped over him, one drawing a scalping knife from his belt and with the other hand seizing Rupert by the hair.

At that instant consciousness returned. Rupert opened his eyes, and seeing the gleaming knife lifted high in the air, sent up a swift but silent cry to God for help.

The Indian's hold upon his hair suddenly relaxed, and the knife was returned to his belt. He had changed his mind, as he gave his companions to understand in a few words quite unintelligible to Rupert, who was indeed again fast losing consciousness. An answering sentence or two came indistinctly to his hear as sounds from the far distance, then he knew nothing more for a time. How long he could not tell, but on recovering consciousness, he found himself strapped to the back of an Indian pony which was slowly toiling up a steep ascent, a narrow path winding round a mountain. On the right was a rocky wall; on the left was a sheer descent of many hundred feet.

Rupert turned dizzy, sick, and faint as he caught a glimpse of the frightful precipice, the foaming stream and jagged rocks at its base, and but for the thongs that bound him firmly to the back of his steed, he must inevitably have fallen and been dashed to pieces upon them.

He could not in that first moment remember what had befallen him, and he called in a faint voice upon his brother, "Don, where are we?"

No reply, and he called again, more faintly than before, for he was very weak from pain and loss of blood, "Don, Don!"

An Indian's "Ugh!" and a few words in an unknown tongue answered him from the rear.

The sounds were guttural and harsh and seemed to him to command silence.

Instantly he comprehended that he was a prisoner and in whose hands. He was sorely wounded, too, for every movement of his pony gave him exquisite pain; and now memory recalled the events of the afternoon—the chase, the stinging shot, the fall from his horse, then the waking as from a dream, to feel the grasp upon his hair and see the scalping knife held aloft in the air and just ready to descend upon his devoted head.

Question upon question crowded upon his mind. "Where were his late companions, Morton and Smith? Were they killed? Were they prisoners like himself, or had they escaped? Had the train been attacked, and if so, what was the result? Oh, above all, where was Don, the younger brother, over whom he was to have watched with paternal care? He would have defended Don's life and liberty with his own, but alas, the opportunity was denied him.

He thought of his own probable fate. What was there to expect but torture and death? He remembered to have read that the Indians sometimes carried a prisoner a long distance that the rest of their tribe might share the delight of witnessing his dying torments. Rupert shuddered at the thought that this was the fate reserved for him, and feeling very weak, he half hoped he might die on the way to meet it.

Silently he lifted up his heart in prayer to God for help and succor in this, his sore extremity, and that the consolations of God might not be small to the dear ones at home—especially the tender mother—when the news of his sad fate should reach them.

The last gleams of the setting sun lighted up the lofty pathway they were pursuing, but down in that deep valley at the foot of the mountain it was already growing dark. He could see into its depths as he lay with his cheek resting on the neck of the pony, and turning his head, the wall of rock towering on the other side came into view.

He was bound hand and foot and could lift only his head. He seemed to have hardly strength for that, but anxious to learn the number of his captors and whether he was the only prisoner, he made an effort, feebly lifted it, and glanced before and behind him.

He could only see that there were several mounted Indians ahead, and one or more behind him, all fearsome in war paint and feathers. There might be many more at each end of the line—for they were travelling single file along the narrow, winding path—but only a small portion of it came within the line of his vision. And there might be other prisoners, though he saw none.

Even that slight exertion had exhausted him. His head dropped, and again pain of body and distress of mind were forgotten in a long and death-like swoon.

It was night, lighted only by the stars, and the path winding downward, when again he revived for a few moments, shivering and benumbed with cold, weak and faint with hunger and loss of blood, and suffering greatly from the pain of his wounds.

He heard no sound but the rush of a mountain torrent and the clatter of the horses' hoofs over the stony way. He had scarcely more than noted these things when again his senses forsook him.

When next he revived, two of his captors were busy undoing the rope that made him fast to the pony, which was standing stock still on level ground only a few feet from a fire of brushwood that sent up flame and smoke and blazed and crackled with a cheery sound which spoke of warmth for benumbed limbs, while some venison and trout broiling on the coals gave out a savory smell.

Several warriors were grouped about the fire, one giving particular attention to the cooking, the others lounging in picturesque and restful attitudes on the grass.

Rupert was quickly lifted from the pony and laid on the grass beside them with his feet to the fire. Then the cord was taken from his wrists and a bit of the smoking venison put into his hand. He devoured it ravenously, and, his hunger appeased, presently fell into a deep sleep, having first committed himself and dear ones to the care and protection of that God who is everywhere present and almighty to defend and save.

His wounds had been rudely bound up in a way to stanch the flow of blood, it being the desire of his captors to keep him alive, at least for a time. More mercifully disposed than they oftentimes are, and knowing that he was too weak for flight, they left him unbound through the night, merely fastening a cord round each arm and securing the other end to the arm of a stout warrior, one of whom lay on each side of the prisoner.

Rupert had noted as they laid him down that no other white man was in sight. This gave him hope that the rest had escaped, yet he could not know that it was not by death, so the discovery brought small relief to his anxiety of mind on their account.

Morning found him feverish and ill, his wounds very painful. But at an early hour the Indians resumed their line of march with him in the midst, strapped to the pony as before.

It was terrible journey, climbing steep ascents, creeping along narrow ledges of rock where a single false step would have sent them down hundreds of feet to be dashed to pieces upon the sharp points of the rocks below. Now they descended by paths as steep, narrow, and dangerous as those by which they had ascended, and forded streams so deep and swift that the helpless, hapless prisoner was in imminent danger of drowning.

He, poor fellow, was too ill to note the direction in which they were travelling, though he had a vague idea that it was in the main southwesterly.

Besides the difficulties and dangers of the way, he suffered intensely from the pain of his wounds and often from intolerable thirst.

One day he woke as from a troubled sleep to find himself lying on a bearskin in an Indian wigwam, a young girl sitting beside him embroidering a moccasin.

Their eyes met, and hers, large, soft, and dark as those of a gazelle, lighted up with pleased surprise.

"You are better, señor," she said, in low, musical tones and in the Spanish tongue.

Rupert understood her, for he was fond of the languages and had gained a good knowledge of Spanish from Dr. Landreth, who had learned to speak it fluently during his long sojourn in South America.

"Yes," he said faintly in that tongue, "and you have been my kind nurse?"

"It has been happiness to care for the weak and wounded stranger," she said in her liquid tones, "though I little thought he could speak to me in my own language, for you are not my countryman, señor; your face is too fair."

"I am from the United States," he replied. "And you, fair lady?"

"I am a Mexican, a captive among the Indians like yourself," was the mournful reply, tears gathering in the beautiful eyes.

His heart was touched with sympathy, and he

was opening his lips to express it, but with playful authority she bade him be quiet and not waste his feeble strength in talk.

Then she brought him food and drink prepared by her own fair hands, and she fed him, too, for he had scarce strength to feed himself. Directly his hunger was satisfied, and he fell asleep again.

When again he woke, it was night. The stars were shining in the sky, as he could see through the opening in the top of the wigwam left for the escape of smoke, and by their glimmer he could faintly perceive the outlines of dusky forms lying on all sides of him, their quietude and the sound of their breathing telling that they slept.

The impulse came strongly upon him to rise and flee — captivity was so dreadful, liberty so sweet — and it might be that, though so strangely spared up to this time, torture and death were yet to be his portion if he remained.

He started up but only to fall back again in utter exhaustion. He could do nothing to save himself, and there was no earthly helper near, but sweetly to his mind came the opening verses of the forty-sixth psalm, "God is our refuge and strength, a very present help in trouble. Therefore will we not fear, though the earth be removed, and though the mountains be carried into the midst of the sea," and silently committing himself and loved ones — all so far distant — to the care of that almighty Friend, he fell asleep again.

He was quite alone when next he woke, and it was broad daylight, for a bright sunbeam had found its way through the opening in the roof and laid bare to his view the whole interior of the wigwam, with all its filth and lack of the comforts of civilized life.

All was silence within, but from without came the merry shouts and laughter of the Indian children at play. Presently one pushed aside the curtain of skins that served as a door, and a pair of wild black eyes stared Rupert in the face for a moment. Then the curtain fell, and soft, swift retreating footfalls came faintly to his ear.

Not many minutes had passed when it was again drawn aside, and Juanita, the Mexican girl he had seen the day before, stepped within, dropping it behind her.

Her sweet though melancholy smile seemed to light up the forlorn hut as she bade Rupert good morning in her liquid tones, using the Spanish tongue as before, and asked if he could eat the morsel she had brought. Alas, it was not such a breakfast as would have been served him in his own faraway home.

It was a broiled fish, hot from the coals, laid upon a bit of bark and covered with green oak leaves in lieu of a napkin. He thanked her gratefully and asked if she could give him some water with which to wash his face and hands before eating.

Setting his breakfast on the ground beside him, she went out and presently returned with a gourd filled with cold, clear water from a little stream that ran sparkling and dancing down the mountainside but a few yards away.

He first took a long deep draught, for he was suffering with feverish thirst, then laved face and hands, she handing him his own handkerchief, which had been washed in the stream and dried in the sun, to use in place of a towel.

He recognized it and, glancing down at his person, saw that he was attired in the clothes he had on when taken, and that, as they were free from bloodstains, they too must have been washed by some kindly hand and replaced upon him after their cleansing.

"How much I owe you!" he said, looking gratefully at her.

"No, not much," she answered with shy modesty. "Now eat, señor, or your breakfast will be cold."

"I must first rest a little," he returned with a sigh of weariness as he fell back exhausted upon his rude couch.

She caught up several deer and bear skins that lay scattered about, rolled them together, and placed them as a pillow under his head. Then, drawing two small objects from beneath that one on which he had been lying, she held them up to his gaze, asking, "Do you value these, señor?"

"Indeed do I," he cried, stretching out an eager hand. "My precious little Bible and my medicine case! I am thankful beyond expression that they have been preserved to me. How did it happen, señora?"

She explained that she had seen them in the possession of his captor, had begged that they might be given to her, and the Indian, thinking them of little worth, had complied with her request.

He poured out renewed thanks as he took up his Bible and turned over the pages, gazing upon it all the while with loving, delighted eyes.

"An English book, is it not?" she asked, watching him with mingled surprise and curiosity.

"Yes," he said, "the Book of books, God's own holy Word. You have read it in Spanish, señora?"

"The Bible? We are not allowed to touch it. Our church forbids. I never saw one before," she said as she gazed upon it with a kind of awed curiosity and interest.

"A Catholic," he thought. "Perhaps it was for her sake I was sent here. If life be spared me, I will, with God's help, do my best for her."

She broke in upon his thoughts, "Come, señor, eat, or your fish will be quite cold."

When Juanita left him, carrying away with her the remains of his repast, an old squaw paid him a short visit, looking curiously at him and grunting out several questions which were utterly unintelligible to him. He could only shake his head and feebly sign to her that he did not understand.

She left him, and he took up his book but found the light was not sufficient to enable him to read, for it was a very small edition which he had been accustomed to carry in his pocket.

He was heartily glad when Juanita again appeared, this time with the moccasin she was embroidering in her hand, and seated herself at this side.

"I am stronger today, señora," he said, "and can listen and talk. Tell me of yourself."

To that she answered briefly that she was an orphan, both parents having died while she was yet a mere infant; that she had lived in the family of an uncle, where she was made to feel her poverty and dependence, and her life rendered

far from happy; that some months ago the
Indians had made a raid upon her uncle's ranch,
killed him and all his family and had carried her
off a prisoner to this mountain fastness; and that
she had been adopted by one of their chiefs,
Thunder-Cloud, and had no hope of any better
fate than a life spent among the savages.

"Too sad a fate for one so beautiful, señora,"
Rupert said. "But do not despair. God, who res-
cued Daniel from the lions' den, and Jonah from
the belly of the whale, can save us also even from
this stronghold of our fierce foe."

"I know nothing of the occurrences you speak
of," she said, "and I dare not venture to address
any petition directly to the great God. But I pray
daily to the Blessed Virgin and the saints to have
pity upon a poor friendless girl and restore me to
my country and my people, though, alas, I know
not of one in whose veins flows a single drop of
my blood."

"Ah, señora," replied Rupert, "you need not
fear to approach the great God in the name of His
dear Son, our Lord and Saviour Jesus Christ. He
bids us do so, and tells us that He is the bearer
and answerer of prayers."

He paused, closed his eyes, and lifted up his
heart in silent supplication for her and for himself.

She thought he slept, and sat very quietly, busy
with her embroidery and waiting for him to wake
again.

At length he opened his eyes and asked her if she
knew what fate the Indians had reserved for him.

She told him a council had been held while he
lay unconscious from his wounds; that there was

a heated discussion, some of the braves being set upon putting him to a torturing death, while others would have held him for ransom. But finally Thunder-Cloud, whose shot had brought him to the ground, had claimed him as his peculiar property and declared his intention to adopt him as his son. "So," she concluded, "you, señor, need have no fear of being slain by any of the tribe, unless caught in an attempt to escape."

"God be praised!" he cried, with clasped hands and uplifted eyes, "for life is sweet so long as there is a possibility of future restoration to home and loved ones."

"You will attempt to escape?" she asked with a look of apprehension. "It will be very dangerous, señor, for they are terribly fierce, these Apaches."

He looked at her with a faint smile. "I am far too weak to think of it now, but one day, when I have recovered my health and strength, I may find an opportunity."

"And I shall be left alone with them as before," she said with a touchingly mournful cadence in here exquisite voice.

"You must fly also, señora," he answered. "I think it is to you I owe my life, for have you not been my faithful nurse through I know not how long a sickness? Then how could I be so ungrateful as to leave you here in captivity while I seek home and freedom for myself?"

"You have home and kindred, father and mother perhaps, señor?" she asked inquiringly, the soft eyes she fixed upon his face wistful and dim with unshed tears.

"Ah," he answered with emotion, "the thought

of their anguish when they shall learn my fate doubles my distress."

"Then," she sighed, "it is better to be alone in the world, like me, with none to care whether you live or die."

"Nay, sweet lady, there is one who cares very much, though he has known you so short a time," he said with a grateful look. "One who would feel doubly desolate were you to leave him here alone with his captors."

CHAPTER SIXTEENTH

Calamity is man's true touchstone.

"YOU HAVE TALKED too much, señor," Juanita said with concern, noting the look of utter exhaustion that came over his face with the last words. "I am but a poor nurse to have allowed it. Your lips are parched, too," she added, dropping her work and gliding from the tent to return a moment later with a gourd full of the cold, sparkling water from the mountain stream.

She raised his head and held the cup to his lips.

He drank with feverish eagerness.

As Rupert lay back upon his couch again, Juanita remarked that his wounds must be painful and in need of dressing, adding that Light-of-the-Morning, Thunder-Cloud's wife, who had great knowledge of the virtues of many plants and roots growing in that region, would soon come in and dress them with a certain kind of leaf that was famed among the Indians for its healing qualities, and had already worked wonders for him.

"And she has been dressing my hurts all these days?" asked Rupert.

"Yes."

"Ah, how long have I lain here, señora?"

"Three weeks, señor," she answered, and at that moment the old woman he had seen before came in bearing a bark basket filled with the healing leaves.

Juanita withdrew to the far side of the wigwam and seated herself with her back toward them while Light-of-the-Morning did her work.

The task was performed a trifle roughly but with dexterity and skill, and the applications proved very cooling and soothing to Rupert's wounds, which before had tortured him with a sensation of dryness and burning heat.

He returned warm thanks, Juanita acting as interpreter.

The squaw nodded, her grim features relaxing in a slight smile, as of pleasure, that her labors were appreciated. Then, pointing to Rupert's medicine case lying by his side, she asked what it was.

Juanita repeated the query in Spanish and translated Rupert's answer into Apache, which she had learned to speak with tolerable fluency.

The squaw then asked for some medicine for a sick child in the camp, whose ailment baffled her skill.

Rupert was a good druggist and had sufficient knowledge of medicine to prescribe for the child when he had heard what were the symptoms. Also, the proper remedy was in his case, and he gave it. The result was satisfactory and raised him in the esteem of the whole village.

Squaws, papooses, a few lads and young girls, and a sprinkling of old men were all that were in it at this time, the braves having gone again upon the warpath. This Rupert learned from Juanita.

In a few days he was able to crawl out from the wigwam and lie on a bearskin, which she laid for him underneath a spreading tree. He found the pure mountain air very delightful and invigorating, and from that time his recovery was rapid.

He was soon able to sit up a part of the day and amuse himself with whittling bits of soft wood, making whistles for the little Indian boys and a variety of toys for the girls—tiny chairs, tables, spoons, knives and forks—which greatly delighted them.

Thus he made friends of the children and also of their mothers, while to his generous nature it was a great satisfaction to be able to give such pleasure to these children of the desert.

Also, as he picked up their language, he tried to tell them the old, old story so dear to every Christian heart. To Juanita he was able to tell it at once, and often as she sat by his side during his convalescence, he read to her passages from his Bible, stopping now and then to give an explanation or answer a question, for she listened with interest and a desire to fully comprehend.

That his Bible had been spared to him was a source of deep joy and thankfulness, such comfort did he find in its many great and precious promises.

His heart was often oppressed with sadness as he thought of Don and longed to know his fate, or of the dear ones at home and the distress they would undoubtedly feel on account of his disappearance. He supposed the report would be that he had been killed by the Indians, and he pictured to himself his mother's anguish on hearing the terrible tidings, his father's also, for he knew that to both, their children were very near and dear.

When overwhelmed by these sorrowful reflections, his own comfort was in prayer to Him who is mighty to save, and who, he doubted not, was able both to give consolation to his loved ones and to deliver him from the hands of his foes.

His situation was not an enviable one at the first, but it became less so upon the return of the braves, most of whom regarded him with scowls and looks of hate.

He gave them back pleasant looks, was on the watch to do them any little service in his power, but avoided them when he could without offense. As time went on he found opportunities to win their goodwill.

From his youth he had made a practice of learning all that he could on every subject and about every kind of work that came his way, and now he found use for some kinds of knowledge that most lads would think it beneath them to acquire. He was not only an expert whittler but was equally accomplished as a cook, and he taught the squaws to make savory dishes that the braves, their husbands and sons, loved, thus winning favor for himself.

Yet it seemed not altogether good policy, for finding him so useful, they were the more determined never to part with him. And while treating him well in other respects, they kept him a close prisoner in that little mountain fastness, watching with vigilance his every movement and never suffering him to go out of sight of the village.

Still, Rupert never for a moment faltered in his

determination to effect his escape. But while constantly on the alert for an opportunity, he was extremely careful to do nothing to excite suspicion that such was his purpose.

It was, however, no secret from Juanita, who was to share the attempt whenever made. And frequently when alone, plans for flight, the direction it should take, and what provision could be made for it formed the principal theme of their conversation.

Neither knew exactly where they were, but Rupert had an idea that their nearest route toward civilization would lie in a southeasterly direction and take them into Texas.

He had no means of determining the matter, nor could he for a long time do anything more than think and plan.

In the meanwhile, he tried to be useful in every way to those about him, especially Juanita.

He taught her to speak and read English, using his Bible as his textbook. It was the only one at hand, but it proved sufficient. He found her deplorably ignorant of almost everything but embroidery and music—for which she possessed remarkable talent—but managed, in the course of the three years they spent in the wild together, to give her a great amount of general information—drawing maps in the sand for her instruction in geography and history, using the heavens at night to assist in giving her a knowledge of astronomy, the plants and flowers to which they had access to teach her the rudiments of botany.

Juanita proved an apt pupil, bright and interesting, readily catching an idea and retaining it in her memory, all the more easily, doubtless, because she dearly loved her teacher.

She was very young, had seen nothing of the world, and in her artless simplicity made her affection quite apparent to its object. But he had no difficulty in returning it, and before they had been six months together, they had come to a full understanding and were plighted lovers.

Then Rupert drew bright pictures of his home—the home to which he hoped one day to take her—and of his father and mother, brothers and sisters, all of whom he said would welcome and love her as one of themselves.

But one year and then another rolled slowly away, while deliverance seemed no nearer than the first, and oftentimes their hearts were sick with hope deferred.

It was harder for Rupert than for Juanita, for he whom she had with her was all she had to love, while he, though fondly attached to the lovely girl sharing his captivity, was separated from many who were also very dear to his heart and who must, he knew, be suffering much distress of mind on his account.

Then, too, the enforced inactivity in business matters was very trying to him, while she knew nothing of it.

He was her world, and she had him there. Yet she did not enjoy life with the Indians and longed to return to civilization for her own sake, and still more for his.

Besides, they were at times in great danger when their captors were excited by drink or preparations to go upon the warpath, or upon the return of the braves from such an expedition, either exultant from victory or depressed and angered by defeat.

At length, in the third year of Rupert's captivity, the vigilance of the Indians began to relax somewhat. They thought their prisoners had become enamored of their wild life and would hardly care to risk an attempt to escape, knowing, as they undoubtedly did, that if recaptured, torture and death would be almost sure to follow. So, Rupert and Juanita would occasionally find themselves free to ramble through the extent of the valley and even to climb some of the nearer hills and mountains.

Hope now revived in their breasts, and was quickened before long by a fortunate discovery: They one day came upon some small nuggets of gold, which they carefully secreted about their persons with the joyful thought that it would help them on their contemplated journey.

Then, some weeks later, Rupert picked up a stone which he felt confident was a diamond. This, too, he secreted with the greatest care, sewing it securely upon the inner side of the deerskin hunting shirt which he now wore day and night, and letting no one but Juanita know of its existence. From her he had no concealments, for their interests were one and the same.

They now watched more eagerly than ever for the longed-for opportunity, but weeks and months dragged on their weary way, and it came not.

Another winter, with its suffering from cold and storms from which they were but poorly protected in the rude huts of the Indians, passed slowly by, spring opened, and once more the leaves went forth upon the warpath.

Seated together upon a ledge of rock on the side of a mountain overlooking the Indian village and forming part of the barrier shutting in the little valley from the outer world, Rupert and Juanita watched the departure of the Apache chiefs and braves, fearsome in their warpaint and feathers. And as the last of them disappeared in the defile that formed the sole entrance to this natural mountain fastness, Rupert, turning to his companion, said, in tones of half tremulous eagerness and excitement, "Juanita, love, this is our opportunity. I doubt if we shall ever have a better."

"What mean you, Rupert?" she asked in some surprise. "What will prevent Light-of-the-Morning from watching our every moment as vigilantly as ever? And does not old Crouching Wildcat keep guard day and night at the only entrance to the valley, and is he not constantly armed and ready to shoot us down if we so much as approach the spot where he stands sentinel?"

"All quite true," returned Rupert, "yet I have a plan. Listen, maiden mine, while I unfold it. It is that today and tomorrow we make, quietly and unobserved, every preparation in our power, then that you make a quantity of that savory venison stew that both Light-of-the-Morning and Crouching Wildcat delight in, adding a little white powder which I shall give you. Let them both sup upon it, and they will sleep soundly for some hours—so soundly that we may steal from our wigwams, join each other at the old warrior's side, and pass out of the valley unmolested and unnoticed by him."

"And they will wake again and suffer no harm from the powder?" she asked.

"Yes," he said. "You know, Juanita, I would not murder them even to gain liberty for myself and you. The powder will cause them to sleep heavily for a time, and perhaps make them sick for some hours after, but it will do them no permanent injury."

The girl's face grew radiant. "Oh," she cried, clasping her hands in ecstasy, "how sweet, how delightful to be free! But why not tonight? Why should we wait another day?"

"That when our flight is discovered the braves may be too far away for a messenger to reach them with the news in time for them to overtake us."

"Ah, yes. You are much wiser than I; you think of everything."

The braves were quite gone. The last faint echo of their horses' hoofs had died away far down the pass, and the squaws and children, who had been watching their departure, scattered to their work or play.

Juanita sighed, then said with a shudder, "How many bloody scalps shall we see dangling aloft from their spears when they come back?"

"Please God, we shall not be here to behold the horrible, sickening sight," said Rupert. Then, taking her hand in his, he added, "Juanita, you should be my wife before we start upon our journey."

She glanced up into his face half shyly, flushing rosy red. "But how can that be?" she asked timidly. "There is no priest here to unite us."

"We will marry ourselves by Friends' ceremony," he said and then explained it to her, for she had never heard of it before.

"I fear I shall not feel married," she remarked in a tone of doubt and hesitation.

"I have the same feeling," he said, "particularly because we have no witnesses. But it is the best we can do now, and as soon as we can, we will be remarried by a minister. "Juanita," he began, tightening has clasp of her hand, "I take you to be my wife and promise to be to you a true, faithful, and loving husband till death do us part."

The beautiful eyes filled with glad tears. "And I," she said in low, musical tones, "take you, Rupert, to be my lawful and wedded husband, and promise to be to you a true, loving, faithful, and obedient wife."

He put his arm about her and drew her into a close, tender embrace, imprinting a long and ardent kiss upon the rich red lips. "We are one, love," he whispered, "and what God hath joined together shall no man put asunder."

After some further discussion of their plans, they separated and by mutual consent were seen together less than usual during that day and the next, so fearful were they of arousing suspicion of their design to attempt an escape.

But late in the afternoon of the second day, Rupert contrived to give Juanita the little morphine powder which she was to administer to Light-of-the-Morning and Crouching Wildcat, and to do it unperceived by any of the Indians.

Juanita hastily concealed it, fastening it into the folds of her tunic with a pin.

There were but few cooking utensils in the Indian village, but Light-of-the-Morning was the proud possessor of a little iron pot carried off by the braves in one of their raids upon their white neighbors, and of this Juanita was allowed to make use in preparing the savory stew of which Rupert had spoken.

When she proposed doing so tonight, the old squaw nodded consent with a smile of approval.

The newly made bride went cheerily to work, moving about with her accustomed grace and softly humming a snatch of song, yet with a quaking heart as she thought of the risk she and Rupert were now to run.

As he and she were to partake of the meal, she also broiled venison and fish over the coals, and baked bread, making her dough into long, slender rolls, which she then twisted round and round a stick. That she stuck into the ground close to the fire and so baked the bread, now and then pulling up the stick and replanting it with another side to the fire.

Light-of-the-Morning sat watching her with a look of great satisfaction, evidently enjoying the feast in anticipation.

At length all was ready, and Juanita began to despair of an opportunity to carry out her design, when the squaw supplied it by seizing a gourd and going for water for the meal.

She had scarcely dropped the curtain of the wigwam behind her before Juanita had snatched the powder from its hiding place and poured it in the stew, turning pale as she did it, for so much depended upon the success of the measure!

And it was an anxious moment to both herself and Rupert when Light-of-the-Morning first tasted of the medicated dish. She paused, tasted again, and remarked that it was not quite so good as usual and had a slightly bitter taste, that Juanita must have been careless and let it scorch. But to their great relief, she went on to make a hearty meal of it, not seeming to notice that neither of them touched it.

There was a good deal left, and Rupert surreptitiously carried it off to Crouching Wildcat, who received the attention with satisfaction and devoured the food with great gusto, apparently never noticing the unusual taste of which the squaw had complained.

Although but little past sunset, the village was already quiet, scarcely anyone, old or young, to be seen moving; for as a rule they kept early hours there.

Juanita had purposely delayed the evening meal in Thunder-Cloud's wigwam, rather to the displeasure of its mistress, whose appetite had grown very keen while waiting. That was a good thing for the success of the young people's plans, for she ate very heartily and almost immediately threw herself down on her couch of skins and fell into a deep sleep.

It was thus Rupert found her on bringing back the vessel in which he had carried Crouching Wildcat his portion.

Juanita sat beside the couch, gazing upon the sleeper with bated breath, her hands folded in her lap, her whole frame trembling with excitement.

As Rupert pushed aside the curtain and

entered, she looked up at him and laid her finger upon her lips.

He smiled and nodded, then stooped and whispered in her ear, "All is already quiet. I think we may set out as soon as it is dark enough to gain the entrance of the pass unperceived. Come then, love, you will find me there."

Her speaking eyes gave the promise he sought, and with a parting, half-regretful glance at the old squaw, who had always been kind to him and Juanita also, he left the wigwam.

Withdrawing to a short distance, he knelt in the shadow of a tree and poured out his soul in fervent prayer for guidance and help in this perilous undertaking.

The shades of evening were falling fast as he rose from his knees. He sent one swift glance around to make sure that no human eye was near enough to watch his movements, and satisfied of that, walked with rapid yet noiseless step toward the foot of the mountain that shut in the valley on the nearest side.

Ascending a little way, he came to a ledge of rock. Stooping down and thrusting aside the overhanging branches of a wild vine that concealed a little hollow, he took from thence a bundle of jerked buffalo meat and venison, which he had collected in preparation for the flight, and with it in his hand rapidly retraced his steps.

He paused beneath the tree he had just left to take another reconnoitering glance and was startled to find someone leaning against it. The faint outline of the figure was barely perceptible in the gathering darkness, but only for an instant. The next he knew, it was Juanita, and his arm stole round her waist.

"My love, my darling," he whispered, "does your heart fail you?"

"No, beloved, not while you are with me and lead the way," she answered softly.

"Come, then. I think they are all asleep, and it is quite dark. Now is our time," he said, taking her hand and leading her onward.

Both had learned to walk with the Indian's noiseless tread. They wore moccasins, and there was no sound of footsteps as they pursued their silent way to the mouth of the pass.

Before they reached it, the loud snoring of the sentinel told them there was no danger of molestation from him. He lay prone upon the ground, so soundly asleep that Rupert was able to divest him of his arms without waking him.

The gun, powderhorn, and shot bag were Rupert's own, which had been taken from him at the time of his capture, so that the most scrupulous conscience could have seen no wrong in his taking possession. Though, indeed, had they not been his own, he would have thought it no robbery under the circumstances.

He was exceedingly glad to find both bag and horn well filled, for on that largely depended his ability to supply food for himself and Juanita on the long journey that lay before them before they could reach the confines of civilization.

Attaching those two articles to the belt that confined his hunting shirt about the waist, and putting the gun over his shoulder, with the bag of dried meat hung upon it, he took Juanita's hand in his again and led her up the pass, away from the scene of their captivity.

It was very dark in that narrow defile with the mountains towering far above them on each side, and the way was narrow, rough, and stony. Again and again they stumbled and were near falling, yet held each other up. But they pressed patiently, determinately onward, without pause or exchange of word or syllable, till they reached the end and came out upon a wide-open plain.

The newly risen moon, flooding it with silver light, showed them something of its nature and extent. It was treeless and, except along the margin of a stream that crossed it, a sandy waste. It did not look inviting, but across it lay the path to freedom, home, and friends.

They paused but a moment to recover breath and take in the view by one sweeping glance from side to side, then pressed forward more rapidly than had been possible in the darkness of the defile from which they had just emerged.

"Thank God, there is no foe in sight!" exclaimed Rupert. "But we must make all haste across this plain, for if pursued, we can be seen from a great distance. Also let us gain yonder stream as quickly as possible and walk in the water to destroy the scent of our footsteps, and leave no mark of a trail by which we can be tracked."

"Yes, yes," panted Juanita. "Oh, let us hasten."

"My poor darling, you are already almost spent," Rupert said tenderly. "Lean on me. If I were but free of the gun and bag of meat, I would take you in my arms."

"No, no," she returned with a little pleased laugh. "I should not allow it. I am but a trifle out of breath, that is all, my best of husbands."

"I am happy to hear it," he said, "for I fear your strength will be sorely tried before we can reach a place of safety. Draw your blanket more closely about you, for the night wind has full sweep across this open plain, and its cold is piercing."

They had both been forced to adopt the Indian style of dress. Juanita had neither cloak nor shawl but wore a blanket wrapped about her shoulders, after the manner of the squaws.

She drew it closer, took Rupert's arm, and they sped swiftly over the plain, the sense of impending danger lending them unnatural strength and speed.

They reached the stream and followed its course for some miles, keeping just within the water's edge, then left it for a more direct route, which brought them, about daylight, to a dense forest.

Being now utterly spent with fatigue, they were obliged to stop and take some rest. Rupert spread his blanket at the foot of a tree, made Juanita lie down upon it, and carefully covered her with her own. "My poor child, how very weary you are!" he sighed in tender accents.

"Ah, if I could but provide a cup of hot coffee and good warm breakfast for your refreshment! But I have nothing to offer you but this dried venison, and I dare not even kindle a fire to dry your wet feet, lest the smoke should attract the attention of our fearsome foes."

"Ah," she said with a determined effort to be cheerful, and giving him a sweet, bright smile, "we will not mind such trifles, if only we may escape being recaptured. Give me a bit of the venison; I can eat it with appetite."

They rested and slept where they were for some hours. Then, late in the afternoon, they started on again through the forest, trying to keep a southeasterly direction and guided by the sun, of which they caught occasional glimpses between the tall treetops.

About the time of his setting, they came out upon a little opening in the forest. Here they halted, made another meal upon the dried meat, then lay down and slept until the moon rose, when they pressed on again, guided by her light.

So, for many weeks they journeyed on, the sun guiding them by day, the moon and stars at night. Sometimes, when clouds covered these from view, they were obliged to lie by for hours or days and were often compelled to do so from utter weakness and weariness, drinking water from the streams and satisfying their hunger upon fish caught in them, or such game as Rupert was able to bring down with his gun or catch in snares laid for them when he and Juanita stopped for a night's rest.

He kept an account of the days of the week and was careful to observe the rest of the Sabbath. He had brought his Bible with him, and the greater part of the day would be passed in the study of its pages and prayer to that God who is everywhere present and able to deliver from all dangers and fears. Rupert and Juanita were in a situation to feel very sensibly the need of His protecting care, for danger from wild beasts and roving bands of Indians threatened them on every side. Venomous reptiles, too, often lay in their path, and they were not seldom assailed by both hunger and thirst, sometimes travelling many, many miles without finding either food or water.

CHAPTER SEVENTEENTH

Sir, you are very welcome to our house:
It must appear in other ways than words,
Therefore I scant this breathing courtesy.

—SHAKESPEARE

IT WAS LATE in the afternoon of a sultry August day that our poor travellers, footsore and weary, reached a great cattle ranch in Texas, owned and occupied by a family of the name of Baird, who had emigrated from Ohio years before.

Their large, comfortable house, separated from the road by a wide, grassy yard and flower garden, was the first civilized dwelling Rupert and Juanita had seen since their capture by the Indians, and their pulses quickened with joy at the sight.

Mrs. Baird was getting supper for her husband and sons, all of whom were in the field with the cattle. Turning from the fire where she was broiling chickens, baking biscuit, and frying potatoes, she caught sight of two forlorn figures coming up the garden path.

"Injuns!" she cried aloud, as, pale and breathless with fright, she looked this way and that for some weapon of defense, "and me here alone!"

213

But a second glance reassured her. They were nearing the open door, and she could see not only that they were whites but that there was nothing sinister or fierce in the expression of the man's face, while that of the young girl, though pale and travel stained, was winsome and even beautiful.

She stepped forward with a cordial "How d'ye do? Walk in, and sit down, and rest, for you are dreadfully tired, I know," she added, setting out some chairs as she spoke.

"Thank you, madam, indeed we are," Rupert replied, lifting his hat with a courtly bow.

But as they crossed the threshold, Juanita staggered and would have fallen had not he caught her in his arms.

"Oh, my darling, my darling!" he cried in tones of acute distress, "Have food and rest come too late for you?"

"Food and rest?" repeated Mrs. Baird, greatly shocked, "Is she starved? Here, lay her down quick on the lounge in the sitting room, and I'll bring her a glass of milk at once. 'Twon't take me a minute to get it."

With a word of thanks, Rupert followed the good woman's directions and had scarcely done so before she was at his side with the milk.

He raised Juanita's head. Mrs. Baird held the glass to her lips, and noted, with tears of mingled joy and compassion, the eagerness with which it was swallowed.

Then a sudden thought sent her flying from the room to return immediately with a pitcher, from which she filled glasses again and again, first for Juanita, then for Rupert.

"Now," she said, when her pitcher was empty, "you shall both have a good hearty supper in about ten minutes. If you'd like to wash off the dust first, you'll find soap, water, and towels handy out there on the porch. Now I must leave you, or my supper will be all spoiled."

"Oh, Rupert, how good and kind she is!" whispered Juanita with tears I her eyes as their hostess left them alone together. "And she could never suppose from our appearance that we have anything to pay with."

"No, she must be a truly benevolent woman, and a Christian one also, I think. And truly we have great reason to thank our heavenly Father for bringing us to such a one in our sore need," said Rupert, adding, as Juanita made a movement as if to rise, "Lie still, love, I will bring a basin of water to you."

"Please do," she answered, lying down again. "A wash will be very refreshing. Ah, if one only had some clean clothes to put on!"

"That desire also shall be granted before long, my darling," Rupert answered between a tear and a smile, glancing down rather ruefully at the worn and soiled garments of his pretty young wife.

He had shielded her as far as possible from the hardness of their terrible journey, yet he knew that her sufferings had been great — so great that his kind, loving heart bled at the very thought of them.

She had beautiful hair, very fine, soft, glossy and black as the raven's wing, very long and luxuriant, too, when unconfined, falling in a great mass of ringlets below her waist.

Rupert was very proud of it, as well as of her regular and delicate features, her starry eyes, sylphlike form, and graceful movements.

At present she wore here hair in a great coil at the back of her shapely head, held in place by a wooden pin that he had made for her.

"May I take this down and comb it out for you?" he asked, laying his hand caressingly upon it. "But perhaps it would tire you too much."

"Oh no, it would rather be a refreshment," she answered, smiling up at him, "and I shall be much obliged."

So he did, then brought her the water to wash her hands and face.

Meanwhile, Mrs. Baird, busy with her preparations for the evening meal, was full of curiosity in regard to her unexpected guests. "Who can they be?" she questioned with herself, "and where in the world did they come from? It's as plain as day that he's a gentleman and she's a lady; they look it in spite of their odd, shabby dress. And they speak good, pure English in refined tones, though she has a little foreign accent. She looks Spanish, but he's an American; I'm sure of that. Shouldn't wonder if he's from my own state — from that section anyway, for he's neither a New Englander nor a Southerner. But their dress — why, it's nearer Injun than anything else. Well, now I wonder — " she said, and hurrying to the sitting-room door she addressed Rupert:

"If you please, sir, I'd like to ask a question. Have you been among the Injuns?"

"Yes," he said. "We escaped about three

months ago from an Apache village, where we had been prisoners for three years."

"Dear me! How dreadful! And that must have been a long way off. How did you ever get here?"

"Yes, it must be hundreds of miles, and we have walked all the way."

"Oh you poor things!" she cried, the tears coursing down her cheeks. "No wonder you're completely worn out. Your sufferings must have been dreadful."

"They have not been small," Rupert said with emotion, his glance resting pityingly for an instant upon Juanita's wan features. "But as our days, our strength has been, for God is faithful to His promises. And now," he added, with a brightening countenance, "the worst is all over, I trust."

"Yes, indeed. You must stay here till you're quite rested," she said with cordial hospitality. "And as soon as there's a good chance, I'd like to hear your whole story. It can't fail to be interesting."

Turning hastily away with the last word, she seized a tin horn, and going to the back door blew a vigorous blast.

Her husband, three stalwart sons grown to man's estate, and a slender lad of twelve, the youngest and therefore the family pet, came hurrying from the field in answer to the summons.

The wife and mother met them at the threshold, her still fresh and comely face full of excitement. "We have guests," she said.

"Who on earth, mother?" exclaimed Joe, the eldest son, while his father remarked, "They're welcome, whoever they are, if they're honest, decent folks."

"That I'll engage they are!" she answered, "though their clothes are shabby enough. But they're escaped captives from the Apaches, have been travelling through the wilderness for months on foot, and of course are in a very bad plight."

Her announcement was met by various exclamations of surprise and commiseration, according to the characters and dispositions of the speakers.

"Yes," she said, "and of course, father, we'll keep them here till they're rested, poor things, and then help them on their way to their friends, if they have any."

"Of course, of course, wife," answered the man of the house cheerily. "But where are they?"

"In the sitting room," she answered. "Go in and speak to them, won't you? And ask them out to supper; it's just ready."

"I'll do that!" he said, hanging up the towel he had been using.

In another minute he was shaking hands cordially with Rupert, congratulating him on his escape from the Indians, and assuring him and Juanita of their welcome to the hospitalities of the ranch as long as they might be pleased to accept them. "No obligations, young man," he said, interrupting Rupert's expression of thanks. "You'd do the same for me if our situations were reversed, and besides, any decent stranger is a godsend in these lonely parts. And the cost of entertaining, where you have everything on your place and no market for it, is just about nothing. Come, walk out to supper," he added; "it's on the table and best while it's hot."

He led the way, and they followed right willingly, for the smell of the viands was extremely appetizing, and the milk had by no means appeased their hunger.

Mrs. Baird greeted them with a smile, pointed out their seats, and with an inclination of the head toward the younger members of the family, said, "My sons, Mr. —"

"Keith," supplied Rupert, as she paused with an inquiring look at him. "Rupert Keith is my name, and this young lady," glancing at Juanita, "is—"

There was an instant's hesitation, then he added, "my wife," coloring slightly as he spoke.

He was conscious of a furtive exchange of wondering, inquiring glances among his entertainers, but no remark was made.

They all sat down to the table, the father asked a blessing upon the food, and the meal began.

Presently Rupert said, with a frank look into the face of his host, "I must ask to be permitted to explain my hesitation of a moment ago.

"Juanita and I have been fellow captives among the Apaches. They carried her off in a raid into Mexico—her native land. Me that captured on my way from Indiana to California, and we made our acquaintance in the Indian village.

"It was not long before we became lovers, but there was no one there to unite us in marriage. Just previous to making our escape, we married ourselves by Friends' ceremony, as the best we could do. But having had no witness, we do not feel quite satisfied that the knot has been tied as tightly as it ought to be (the reason of my hesitation to claim her as fully mine)," he put in parenthetically and with a look and smile of ardent affection directed to his bride. "And as soon as we can come across a minister, we will get him to tighten it," he concluded with a half-sportive look and tone. Then, more gravely, he inquired, "Is there one in this neighborhood?"

All present had listened with evident interest to his explanation. The father of the family now answered, "None very near, but there's a Methodist minister of the name of Clark, who passes here every other Sunday on his way to a schoolhouse six miles beyond, where he preaches. He generally takes his dinner here, and that will be a good chance for you, if you can wait for it."

"'Twon't be so long, father," remarked his wife cheerily. "This is Friday, and next Sunday is Mr. Clark's day."

"Why, to be sure, so it is!" exclaimed her spouse, turning a beaming face upon Rupert and Juanita.

"We can wait," Juanita said in her liquid tones, speaking for the first time since she had sat down at the table. "I am but poorly prepared so far as regards my dress," she added with blushing cheek and a shy, downward glance at her forlorn attire.

Rupert gave her a tenderly sympathizing look, then turning to their host asked, "Is there any place within reach where clothing may be procured? I have means to pay for it, and we are both, as you see, sorely in need of it."

"The nearest place is twenty miles away, and it's none of the best," was the discouraging reply. "However, we'll see what can be done. Joe can drive you over tomorrow, if you feel like taking the trip, but I should think you'd better rest a few days first."

"Yes, indeed, I should think so," chimed in Mrs. Baird. "Joe can lend him a suit to be married in (they look to be pretty near of size), and I'll find something for the young lady."

"Certainly, certainly!" assented Joe with ready cordiality and a kindly look at Rupert, who was beaming with joy and gratitude.

"You are all exceedingly kind," he said with emotion.

And truly he and Juanita looked in need of such kindly offices. They were dressed almost exactly alike — in full suits of deerskin, moccasins, leggings, and a long loose shirt belted in at the waist, all much worn and soiled with months of constant wear and the dust of travel. On their arrival each had worn a broad-brimmed hat woven by Juanita's deft fingers.

Their entertainers, though eager to hear the story of their captivity and subsequent wanderings, kindly refrained from questioning them till their appetites had been fully satisfied.

At the conclusion of the meal, Juanita was made to lie down again, Mrs. Baird insisting that she must be altogether too tired to sit up. Rupert was given an arm chair, and all the family gathered round him to listen to a lengthened narrative of his experiences from the time of his capture to the present.

Some passages were so moving that there was not a dry eye in the room, and tenderhearted Mrs. Baird sobbed aloud.

When the story seemed to have come to an end, she started up, saying, "Dear me! I've left my dishes standing all this while!" and hastily left the room.

Her husband and sons remained and plied Rupert with questions.

"What have you done with your gun?" asked Ralph, the youngest. "You said you had one that you stole back from that old Wildcat, but I haven't noticed it anywhere round."

"No," Rupert said, "when we came in sight of this house I felt safe in getting rid of the burden of carrying it for a while. Our blankets, too. We were so tired and the sun so hot that they seemed an almost intolerable load, so I hid them in a clump of bushes a little off the roadside, where I knew I could easily find them again."

"That was wise," remarked his host. "We will go for them in the morning."

"Did that old Wildcat and the rest chase after you?" queried Ralph.

"Indeed, my little man, I do not know," replied Rupert. "If so, it was when it was too late for them to overtake us."

"I think you managed splendidly," remarked Tom, the second son.

"I think God helped and took care of us," Rupert said with reverent gratitude.

"And there you are right," said his host. "'Except the Lord build the house, they labor in vain that build it; except the Lord keep the city, the watchman waketh but in vain.'"

"Words of inspiration," Rupert said, recognizing them with a smile of glad content. "I perceive that we are fellow servants of the same divine Master, and much I thank Him for bringing me to the house of one of His followers for a short time of rest."

"And most welcome you are, sir, especially as belonging to Him," returned Mr. Baird heartily. "'Inasmuch as ye have done it unto one of the least of these my brethren, ye have done it unto me.' Those words of His make it a double delight to do any kindness to one of His disciples."

All this time Juanita had been soundly sleeping. Her head had scarcely touched the pillow before she was lost to all that was going on about her.

Mrs. Baird, coming in again, noticed that Rupert seemed very weary.

"You are making Mr. Keith talk too much," she said to the others. "He's fairly tired out and ought to be sleeping this minute. I'll make up a bed directly for you, and one for her," she added, addressing Rupert and glancing toward Juanita with the last words.

"Oh no, do not give yourself the trouble," he hastened to say. "I doubt if either of us could sleep in a bed after being so long used to nothing softer than a bear or buffalo skin spread upon the ground."

Mrs. Baird gave him a puzzled look. "What can I do for you then?" she asked.

"Give me an old quilt or something of the kind, if you have one conveniently at hand, and I will lie on the floor here."

"Yes, I'll get you a quilt and a couple of buffalo robes," she said, "though I' rather give you a good bed. I may make up one for her, mayn't I?"

Rupert smiled and, with a loving glance at Juanita, said, "I really think she would prefer to stay where she is till tomorrow morning. She will probably sleep on till then without moving or so much as opening an eye, she is so very weary, poor thing!"

"And," Mrs. Baird said with a little doubtful hesitation, "you wouldn't rather have separate rooms? I have plenty of them."

"No, she is my wife, and we have been together night and day ever since our escape from captivity, and she has slept close at my side or in my arms. How could I have it otherwise, with the growl of the bear, the savage howl of the wolf, or the scream of the wildcat in our ears, to say nothing of constant danger from roving bands of Indians?"

"Sure enough, sir, and she is your wife! Well, it shall be just as you wish, though it does seem like treating you both very inhospitably."

"Not at all, my dear madam. In fact, neither of us would be willing to get into one of your nice clean beds without a bath and change of raiment, which we cannot have at present."

"Why, yes you can, of course," put in Joe. "We have a bathroom, and I'll supply you with a change of clothes, without waiting for the Rev. Mr. Clark's coming," he added, with a good-humored laugh.

"And I'll do the same by your wife tomorrow morning," said the mother as she hurried away in search of the quilt.

She kept her word, and Juanita appeared at the breakfast table very agreeably metamorphosed by civilized garments, though the calico dress was a little faded and had to be belted in about the waist because it was several sizes too large.

But no attire, however uncouth, could hide the gracefulness of her form and movements or mar the beauty of her face.

"They won't come anywhere near fitting, you are so much more slender than I am," Mrs. Baird had remarked when offering them, "but at least they are sweet and clean as soap and water can make them."

"The best possible recommendation, dear lady," Juanita answered with a joyous smile. "Oh, you do not know how glad I shall be to be clean once more! You could only learn by living in a wigwam for three years and then travelling through the woods and over the mountains and prairies in the one suit, wearing it day and night."

"A great deal more than I should be willing to pay for the knowledge," returned her hostess between a smile and a tear. "You poor young thing! What a fearful time you must have had!"

Rupert's appearance had undergone quite as great an improvement as Juanita's, and the couple exchanged many admiring glances during the meal.

Afterward, when they found themselves alone together for a moment, Rupert, catching Juanita in his arms and giving her a rapturous embrace, exclaimed, "How lovely you are this morning, my darling!"

"You too," she said, laying one small hand on each of his broad shoulders and gazing fondly up into his face.

"It's the clothes—altogether the clothes in my case, I fear," he returned, half laughingly. "Indian attire is none too becoming to me."

"Nor to me," she responded. "It's the change of dress with me as well as with you. But oh, my Rupert, I have always thought you the handsomest of men, even in rude attire!"

"Little flatterer!" he said, laughing and pinching her cheek, yet evidently not ill pleased with the compliment. "That dress is extremely becoming. Really, you are positively bewitching in it."

"Ah, who is the flatterer now?" she cried, clapping her hands and laughing gleefully.

Ralph looked in at the door. "Mr. Keith, father says would you like to come and look at some of our fine cattle, if you are not too tired?"

"Yes, indeed I should, thank you," Rupert answered, letting go of Juanita to follow the boy but turning back again to kiss her goodbye and bid her take all the rest she could.

"Thanks, señor," she returned merrily, "but I feel quite fresh this morning, and I must see if I cannot give a little help to our kind hostess. She seems to have no servant, and our presence here must add to her labors."

"Quite right," he said with an approving smile, "but do not overtax your strength."

Mrs. Baird was not in the kitchen, where Juanita expected to find her, but hearing the light step of the latter, called to her from an inner room.

"Come here, my dear," she said, "and tell me what you think of this."

It was a white dress of fine cambric muslin, its skirt, waist, and sleeves elaborately trimmed with tiny tucks, embroidery, and lace. Mrs. Baird held it up to view, repeating her query, "What do you think of this?"

"That it is very pretty," Juanita answered, examining it closely. "What beautifully fine needlework."

"Yes, it's a dress I had when I was married," remarked Mrs. Baird. "I was a bit of a slender girl then, as you are now. I never wore it much, and after a while I grew too stout for it. I thought of it last night when considering what could be found for you to wear tomorrow, so I've just been rummaging through these bureau drawers in search of it.

"Of course it must be very old-fashioned, and it's very yellow from lying by so long, but there won't be anybody here that knows about the fashions or will mind that it isn't white as it should be. So if you are willing to wear it, just try it on to see if it comes anywhere near fitting. If it does, I'll have it in the washtub in a trice, and I really think it won't look so badly when I'm done with it."

"How very kind you are, dear lady!" exclaimed Juanita, catching Mrs. Baird's hand and kissing it, her face all aglow with delight and gratitude. "It is lovely! And I shall not care at all for the fashion or for a little yellowness, which will make the lace look all the richer."

"Then put it on, my dear," Mrs. Baird said smilingly. "And you need not feel overburdened with gratitude for so small a favor."

It proved not a bad fit, and both thought it would do extremely well without alteration.

"Now if you only had decent pair of shoes," remarked Mrs. Baird reflectively. "But those I'm afraid I can't supply, for any of mine would be a mile too large for that pretty little foot of yours."

"Ah! Which would you advise, dear lady, bare feet or these?" Juanita asked with a rueful laugh, casting a downward glance at her worn and soiled moccasins.

"Moccasins!" exclaimed Mrs. Baird, struck by a sudden thought. "You've been so long among the Injuns, have you learned to make them, and could you make yourself a pair if you had the materials?"

"Yes, indeed!" was the eager rejoinder. "For myself and Rupert, too."

"Then you shall have them," said the good woman, beginning to rummage again among her stores. "I have a nice soft doeskin that will be just the thing. Ah, here it is!" she said, pulling it down from a high closet shelf;. "And I have some colored silks you can have for embroidering with, if you like."

"Thank you, oh a thousand thanks!" Juanita said, "but the skin is all I want. I prefer the moccasins plain for this occasion, especially as I can make them up so much more quickly. But may I not first help you with your work? I can wash dishes and sweep and dust and make beds."

"No, no, my dear!" Mrs. Baird said in her bright, cheery way. "You shall do nothing of the kind. It is very kind and thoughtful—your offering to do it—but I really don't need help, and you must sit right down to those moccasins. If you'd like to sit in the kitchen while I'm busy there, I'll be very glad of your company."

Before sunset Juanita's bridal attire was quite ready, and she exhibited it to Rupert's admiring eyes with perhaps as much pride and satisfaction as a city belle might have taken in her silks and satins.

"Mrs. Baird says the dress is old-fashioned and not a good color—" began Juanita.

"But what difference does that make, my sweet?" interrupted Rupert. "Who of us will know the difference? And I am sure you will look very lovely, at least in the bridegroom's eyes, and in fact will be better dressed than he," he added merrily. "I hope you won't be ashamed of him."

"Never, never! I shall be proud, very proud!" she cried, throwing an arm about his neck and laying her head on his breast.

"Not prouder than I of my bride," he said softly, caressing her tenderly.

They were interrupted by the call to supper, and scarcely had the meal begun when a horseman rode up to the gate, dismounted, fastened his horse as if quite at home, then came hurrying up the path toward the open door.

There was simultaneous exclamation from several voices: "Why, there's Mr. Clark." And the whole family rose to greet him with a hearty handshake and words of welcome.

Then Rupert and Juanita were introduced, another plate was added to the table, a chair set up for the new arrival, and he was warmly invited to share their meal.

He was not slow to accept the invitation and did ample justice to the viands, praising them without stint as he ate.

"You're the best cook in the county, by all odds, Mrs. Baird, but the Ohio ladies are very apt to understand the business. I don't believe there's a state in the Union can beat Ohio at that."

"I agree with you there, sir," remarked Rupert. "But I have observed that a man is very apt to think nobody else's cooking quite equal to that of his own mother—a fact partly to be accounted for by the other, that children's appetites are usually keen and their digestion good. There is a great deal of truth in the old saying that hunger is the best sauce."

"Was your mother a native of Ohio, Mr. Keith?" asked Mrs. Baird with a look of interest.

"Yes, madam, my father also. All their children were born there, too, so that we are a family of Buckeyes," he added with sportive look and tone.

"I thought so!" she exclaimed emphatically. "The first hour you were in the house, I said to myself, 'I shouldn't wonder if he were from my own State of Ohio.'"

"But I though I heard you say you came from Indiana, Mr. Keith," spoke up Ralph.

"So I did," returned Rupert pleasantly. "We removed to that state some years ago."

"Fine states both," remarked Mr. Clark. "I've lived in both and ought to know. Now confess, Mrs. Baird, that you are wondering what brought me here today."

"To be ready for preaching tomorrow, I presume," she answered dryly. "But why should I be wondering more than the rest?"

"Oh, woman's curiosity, you know, if you'll excuse the jest, for I really don't believe you're

one bit more curious about it than anybody else
here. Well, I had a funeral to attend this morning
some six or seven miles from this, and then two or
three sick folks to visit a little nearer here, and I
thought it wouldn't be worthwhile to go back
home before Monday. You see, I always feel sure
of a welcome at Baird's Ranch."

"That's right. You need never have the least
doubt of it," said his host. "And we are particularly glad to see you this time, because there's a
job waiting for you here."

"Indeed!" cried the minister, elevating his eye-
brows in surprise. "And what may it be? Has one
of these fine boys of yours selected a wife, and is
he wanting me to tie the knot?"

"Ah, your guess is not very wide of the mark,"
laughed Mr. Baird, "though the wedding will not
be exactly in the family."

"There, father, that will do for the present,"
remarked his wife, perceiving that Juanita was
blushing in a slightly embarrassed way. "We have
the whole evening before us, and it won't take
long to make all the necessary arrangements."

"You have not been long in this part of the
country I presume, sir?" Mr. Clark said inquiringly, addressing Rupert.

"I arrived only yesterday, sir," was the reply.

"Direct from Indiana?"

"No, sir, direct from the Apache country, where
I have been a prisoner for three years."

"Is it possible, sir? You must have had a dreadful experience."

And then questions and answers followed in
rapid succession, Mr. Clark almost forgetting to

eat in the intense interest he felt in the story Rupert and Juanita had to tell, for learning from something said by one of the family that she had shared Rupert's captivity, he catechised her also quite closely.

He was captivated by her beauty and her modest, sensible replies, and being presently able to make a shrewd conjecture as to who were to claim his services that evening, thought Rupert a very fortunate man.

Chapter Eighteenth

I bless thee for the noble heart,
The tender and the true,
Where mine hath found the happiest rest
That e'er fond woman's knew.

— Mrs. Hemans

Mrs. Baird made short work of clearing away the remains of the supper and setting everything to rights. Then, taking two of her sons with her, she repaired to the garden.

All three presently returned laden with flowers, with which they proceeded to ornament the parlor, after setting aside some of the fairest and most fragrant for the adornment of the bride.

"What next, mother?" asked Tom. "You are hardly thinking of having a wedding in the house without refreshments, I suppose?"

"No, I've plenty of cake baked: three kinds—bride, pound, and sponge cakes. Now you boys go to the garden and gather all the finest fruits you can find, while I help the bride to dress."

"Dress?" laughed Tom. "What has she to dress in? Will she put on her Indian toggery again?"

"You'll see when the time comes," said his

233

mother. "Now off with you, and show how well you can do our part."

Mr. Baird had repaired to the front porch with his guests, and an animated conversation was going on there, Mr. Clark and Rupert being the chief speakers, when the good lady of the house appeared among them with the announcement that it was time for every one of them to be dressing for the wedding.

"You know your room, Mr. Clark. I've had your saddlebags carried there, and you'll find everything necessary for making your preparations. Mr. Baird, will you please to attend to Mr. Keith? I shall take care of the bride," she said. And linking Juanita's arm in hers, she led her into the house and to a large, airy bedroom that, with its white-draped windows, dressing table, and bed, looked very suitable for a bridal chamber.

The white dress, the new moccasins, and a profusion of the loveliest flowers were there.

Juanita sent a swift glance about the room, taking in all these details and more (the room seemed pervaded by a simple air of elegance, and its atmosphere was redolent of the sweet breath of flowers). Then, turning to her kind hostess, she threw her arms round her neck, and with quivering lips and eyes full of tears, said, "Oh, how good, how good you are to a poor wayfarer, dear lady!"

"It's very little I'm doing, dear child," said Mrs. Baird, returning the embrace. "I'm afraid it must seem but a forlorn kind of wedding to you, and yet I think you should be a happy bride, for sure I am that if you are not a happy wife, it will not be the fault of the man you are marrying."

"No," cried Juanita, smiles chasing away the tears, "there cannot be another in all the world like my Rupert."

"I must admit that I have taken a great fancy to him," Mrs. Baird said, smiling and stroking Juanita's hair caressingly. "Now, dear, let me help you to dress. I want the pleasure of arranging this beautiful hair and trimming it with flowers. They are the most suitable ornament for a bride, and fortunately we have an abundant supply."

"Yes, I prefer them to jewels," said Juanita.

"My dear, you look lovely!" was the delighted exclamation of the good lady when her labors were completed. "Simple and old-fashioned as the dress is, it becomes you wonderfully. I never saw a bride in the richest white silk or satin look half so beautiful as you do in it."

"Ah, you flatter me, my kind friend!" Juanita said with a blush that enhanced her charms.

"Now sit down for a few minutes while I trim the room with the rest of these roses, lilies, and orange blossoms," said her hostess, "and then I'll go and send Mr. Keith to stay with you till I call you to the parlor."

"Ah, may I not help? I would rather," Juanita said, half imploringly. "Dear lady, you must be quite exhausted with the many labors of the day."

"No, no, not at all," laughed Mrs. Baird merrily. "As my husband often says, I have a wonderful capacity for work. I really do believe it was what I was made for."

"You are never ill?"

"No, never. And what a cause for thankfulness! What earthly blessing greater than good health?"

A little later Rupert came in to find Juanita alone, seated before the window and gazing out upon a beautiful landscape of prairie and forest, with richly wooded hills in the distance.

He stepped lightly across the floor, but her quick ear caught the sound of his footfalls. She turned, rose hastily, and threw herself into his outstretched arms.

"My beautiful! My beautiful!" he said softly, holding her close with tenderest caresses.

"Ah, my love, my love. I would I were ten times more beautiful for your dear sake," she responded, gazing into this face with eyes full of happy tears.

"That would be quite impossible," he said, holding her off a little, the better to view her charms, then drawing her close again to repeat his caresses.

So happy in each other were they that the time did not seem long till they were summoned to the parlor, where the whole Baird family and the minister were in waiting.

It was a short, simple, yet impressive ceremony, and the spectators, though few in number, were very hearty and sincere in their congratulations at its close. Rupert felt that all he needed to complete his happiness was the presence of his parents, brothers, and sisters—all, alas, so far away.

He was very eager to reach home, but so weary were both he and Juanita that he had already decided to accept the kind invitation of these newfound friends to stay some weeks with them. Also, it was absolutely necessary they should make some preparation, in the matter of dress, for a decent appearance in civilized society.

The table spread by Mrs. Baird and her sons with the simple wedding feast of cake and fruits, garnished with a profusion of beautiful, fragrant flowers, presented a most attractive appearance. Nor were its delicacies found less agreeable to the palate than satisfying to the eye.

There was no revel, no intoxicating drink, though a great abundance of delicious lemonade, nor was the feasting prolonged to excess. There was, in fact, more talk than eating and drinking, and at a primitively early hour all had retired, each to his own room.

"At last, love, we know beyond a question that we are truly husband and wife," Rupert said, holding Juanita to his heart with tenderest caresses. "Does the certainty add to your happiness, as it does to mine?"

"Yes," she murmured, softly. "Oh, I am happier than ever before in all my life!"

"Ah, it makes my heart glad to hear it! How proud I shall be to show my little wife to the dear ones at home. I hope to have an opportunity on Monday to send them a few lines to tell that I am yet alive and hope to be with them in a few weeks."

He availed himself of that opportunity, writing to Dr. Landreth to break the news to his parents, but the letter never reached its destination. Hence, the intense surprise of his relatives when he arrived among them.

The remainder of the journey was performed in comparative comfort. Rupert bought a pair of stout mules and a roomy wagon, which he and the hospitable Bairds stocked with everything necessary for a journey of several hundred miles through a sparsely settled country.

In this the young couple travelled to New Orleans, stopping at night at some village, farmhouse, or ranch, when any such shelter was near, at other times unharnessing and tethering their mules and sleeping in their wagon.

The parting with the Bairds was a sorrowful one on both sides, for they had become sincerely attached during the weeks spent together, and it was very unlikely they would ever meet again on earth. Their only consolation was in the strong hope and expectation of a final reunion in another and better world.

Rupert and Juanita set out upon this stage of their long journey very decently attired in garments suitable for the exigencies of that kind of travel and carrying some changes with them.

In New Orleans, they replenished their wardrobes, so that they presented a decidedly fashionable and stylish appearance; sold the wagon and mules; and took passage on a Mississippi steamer bound for St. Louis.

The trip up the river seemed really restful after the far more toilsome mode of travel they had practiced for so long. They made some pleasant acquaintances, too, and altogether greatly enjoyed the voyage, with its return to the usages of civilized life.

They stayed but a few hours in St. Louis, then hurried on to Pleasant Plains by the nearest and most rapid route, for Rupert was in a fever of impatience to reach home and the dear ones from whom he had been so long and sadly parted.

Such was the story told to the assembled family on the morning after their arrival, and of course it was listened to with absorbing and often painful interest and followed up by many questions, now from one and now from another.

It was Annis who asked, "What became of your diamond, Ru?"

"Did I say positively that it was a diamond?" he asked in a sportive tone.

"No, I believe not. But what did you do with it?"

"Sold it, little sister; sold it for five thousand dollars."

There was an exclamation of delight from all present except Juanita, to whom the fact was no news.

"Why, my good brother, you seem to have made quite a speculation out of your misfortune in being captured and held prisoner so long," laughed Dr. Landreth.

"Yes," Rupert said with an ardent look of love directed at his bride. "I found a treasure there that I could have found nowhere else and therefore do not regret all I have suffered. Though I would the suffering had been mine alone," he added with a tender glance at his mother's worn face and a perceptible tremble in his manly tones.

"Never mind, my dear boy," she said, laying her hand affectionately upon his arm and gazing with all a mother's love and pride into his handsome face. "None of us need care for them now that they are all over and we have you safe among us once more."

"In fine, vigorous health, too, I should say, from your appearance," added the doctor.

"Yes, Charlie, your prescription has worked wonders," Rupert replied with a happy laugh. "I never felt better in my life."

"And you are quite a rich man," the doctor went on merrily. "Your business here has thrived and increased under my fostering care, so that there are a few thousands in the bank to add to those you have brought with you. And besides, the fine business is ready for you to step into again this very day, if you like."

"Charlie, how can I thank you?" Rupert exclaimed with emotion, grasping the doctor's hand with brotherly warmth.

"No thanks needed, Ru," returned the doctor laconically. "Don, my boy," he said, wheeling round upon him, "I don't believe one of us has asked what success in the search for gold you have to tell of."

"No," said the mother, "we were so glad to get sight of his face that we never thought of the gold."

Don gave here a loving smile. "And I," he said, "have been so taken up with the happiness of being with you all again, and the return of my brother, 'who was dead and is alive again, was lost and is found,' that I have not thought of it myself. I have been moderately successful, so that I have enough to give me a fair start in business."

"I'm very glad, Don," said Rupert. "And if you shouldn't have quite enough, you won't be too proud to take a little help from your older brother, will you?"

"Or your brother-in-law?" supplemented the doctor.

"Or your father?" Mr. Keith added with an affectionate look and smile. "I am abundantly able and have, perhaps, the best right."

Don's face beamed with happiness. "Thank you all," he said.

"No, I shouldn't be too proud to accept help from any of you, father especially, but I hope not to need it."

"But, Rupert," said Wallace, inquiringly, "I suppose you had to use a part of your five thousand for travelling expenses?"

"No, you needn't suppose any such thing, my good brother," replied Rupert with a good-humored laugh. "The gold I told you Juanita and I picked up was more than sufficient for that and all other expenditures—for clothing and so forth—in fact, we still have a few hundreds of it left."

"Fortunate creatures that you are!" said Zillah. "And yet I don't think ten times what you have would pay for that long captivity among the Indians."

"No," said Rupert, "I would not voluntarily endure it again for that—or twice that—though now that it is over, I am not sorry to have had the experience. Are you for your share of it, love?" he said to Juanita, who was sitting by his side.

"Ah, my husband," she said, lifting to him eyes beaming with love and happiness, "I can never, never regret anything that brought us together!"

"What beautifully correct English Juanita speaks," remarked Mildred admiringly.

"Yes, I think so," said Rupert, "and take all the credit to myself, since I have been her only teacher. She could not speak a word of it when we first met."

"He first stole my heart," said Juanita with a low, musical laugh, "and then it was not so difficult to make me understand and speak his language."

"No," said Rupert; "if there was any theft, it was on your side. You robbed me of my heart with the first glance of your lovely eyes, so that when I got possession of yours, it was only a fair exchange, which, according to the proverb, is no robbery."

Juanita looked at him with pretended reproach in her beautiful eyes. "He always gets the better of me when we quarrel like this. He always will have the last word."

"Ah, but you shouldn't let him," Zillah said with a merry look at her husband. "Wallace knows better than to expect it always. Don't you, dear?"

"Oh yes, of course," laughed Wallace. "But for all that, I'm not apt to stop till I've freed my mind, and sometimes my wife is wise enough not to answer back unless with soft words or a merry jest that conquers my inclination to be disagreeable."

"She's a very nice, wise little woman," remarked the doctor, "yet, I think, excelled to some extent by her elder sister," he added, glancing at Mildred as he spoke.

"Probably the possessive pronoun has not a little to do with that opinion, Charlie," Mildred said with a happy smile.

"Rupert," said Don, "did you never lose your

way while crossing those almost boundless Texas prairies?"

"Once we did," replied Rupert, "but finding a compass after some little search, we were able to go on in the right direction."

"A compass?" cried Annis. "What sort of compass could be found out there?"

"It is a little plant which grows there, can always be found, and under all circumstances, in all kinds of weather—sunshine, rain, or frost—invariably turns its leaves and flowers to the north. Mr. Baird pointed it out to me and told me this about it before we left his ranch."

"What a wonderful provision of nature!" exclaimed Wallace.

"How kindly God provides for all the needs of His creatures," said Mrs. Keith.

Silence fell upon them for a moment. It was broken by an exclamation from Juanita.

"What a happy family, my Rupert! How many brothers and sisters, and all so kind and loving to each other."

"And these are not all, my Juanita," he said. "Ah, if only Ada and Cyril were here!" he said, turning to his mother as he spoke.

"Your father has already written for Cyril to come home to see his long-lost brothers," she said, "but Ada we can hardly hope to see for a year or two yet."

"Is she happy?" he asked.

"Very happy in her chosen work, as well as in her husband and two sweet children."

"Dear girl," he murmured. "I trust she will have many stars in her crown of rejoicing. You, too, mother. What a good work you have done in training her for hers."

"To God be all the glory," she said. "Without His blessing, all my teachings would have availed nothing. And greatly as I miss my dear daughter, I feel that He has highly honored me in making me the mother of a devoted missionary of the cross.

"Ah, Rupert, you have had an opportunity to do a like work for the Master while an involuntary dweller among a heathen people."

She looked at him inquiringly as she spoke.

"Yes," he said, "and I made some effort to improve it. I told the old, old story to all whom I could get to listen, and sometimes I thought their hearts were touched. I trust the seed sown may someday spring up and bring forth fruit, though I shall know nothing of it till we meet before the great white throne.

"There was one—an old man, who was ill a long while, dying of consumption—of whom I have strong hope.

"I did what I could to relieve his physical suffering, and he was very grateful. That made him the more willing to listen to my talk of the evil of sin, the danger of eternal death, and God's appointed way of salvation.

"At first he heard me with apparently perfect indifference, but after some time, he became deeply convicted of sin, and at length, as I had reason to believe, sincerely converted.

"'Was it for me, for *me*? Did He die to save *me*?' he asked again and again, the tears falling fast from his aged eyes. 'And His blood cleanses from all sin, *all sin*?' he repeated over and over again.

Then, holding up his hands, he said, 'These hands are red—red with the blood of my foes. I have taken very many scalps. I have slain men, women, and little children. Can His blood wash away such stains?'

"'Yes,' I said. 'Let me read you the very words from God's own Book.' And I did so, for I had my Bible in my hand.

"'The blood of Jesus Christ His Son cleanseth us from all sin. And He is mighty to save,' I added, then read again from the Book,

"'He is able also to save them to the uttermost that come unto God by Him, seeing He ever liveth to make intercession for them.'

"Then I read again from the Book, 'It is Christ that died, yea, rather that is risen again, who is ever at the right hand of God, who also maketh intercession for us,' and spoke more fully than I had before of the resurrection and of Christ as our Advocate with the Father, the one Mediator between God and man.

"He listened eagerly, hanging upon my words as if he felt that the life of his soul depended upon his full understanding of them.

"And I think he did fully comprehend at last, for such light and peace came into his face as almost transfigured it. And the expression never changed during the few hours that he lived.

"I stayed with him to the end, and it was perfectly calm and peaceful."

Rupert paused, overcome by emotion. Juanita crept closer to him and put her hand in his while her eyes sought his face with a look of sympathy and love.

He pressed the little hand fondly, giving her a reassuring smile. Then, addressing his mother again, he said, "I shall always feel that the salvation of that one soul more than repays all I have suffered in consequence of my capture by the Indians."

"Yes," she said, "it is worth more than the sufferings we have all endured in consequence of that, to us, dreadful event. For they were but temporary, and that soul will live forever."

CHAPTER NINETEENTH

Happy in this, she is not yet so old
But she may learn; happier than this,
She is not bred so dull but she can learn;
Happiest of all is that her gentle spirit
Commits itself to yours to be directed,
As from her lord, her governor, her king.

—SHAKESPEARE

"WHAT DO YOU think of the new member of the family, Cousin Flora?" asked Dr. Landreth.

It was the afternoon of the day succeeding the arrival of Don and Rupert and his wife. Dr. Landreth had a call to the country and had invited Flora to drive with him.

They had left the town behind and were bowling rapidly along a smooth, level road running through woods gorgeous in their autumn robes of crimson and gold, russet, green, and brown.

Flora had been among the listeners to Rupert's story of his and Juanita's captivity and subsequent wanderings, and had, as the doctor noticed at the time, furtively watched Juanita very closely.

"I admire her, of course," was the reply.

247

"But why of course?" he asked.

"You all do. No one could help it, for she is extremely handsome."

Rupert was at that very time asking his mother that same question, having gone to her room and found her there alone.

"I think her sweet and beautiful in appearance and manners," Mrs. Keith answered, smiling up at her tall son as he stood at her side and making room for him on the couch where she sat. "There has not been time for me to form any further judgment," she continued as he accepted her invitation, taking her hand fondly into his, "but I assure you I am disposed to the very most favorable opinion, both because you love her and because of all she has done for you. Perhaps but for her faithful nursing of my wounded boy I should never have seen his dear face again."

Her voice trembled with emotion as she spoke the last words.

"Very likely not, dear mother," Rupert said, supporting her with his arm. "But setting aside the gratitude, which is certainly her due, from me at least, I am sure you will soon learn to love her for her many very lovable qualities."

"I do not doubt it, my son. And it rejoices my heart to see how great is your mutual love. I trust it may but increase with years, as has your father's and mine."

"I hope so indeed, mother. It has always been very evident to me that you and my father loved each other dearly. I do not remember ever to have heard either one address an unkind word to the other."

"No," she said. "Your father has been the best of husbands to me always."

After a little pause she added, "Has your wife any education, Rupert?"

"Not much besides what I have contrived to give her myself in the three years we have been together," he said. "But I have really succeeded in giving her a good deal of general information orally and have taught her to read English, using my Bible as a textbook, and to write, using a pointed stick and the sand.

"I had thought of placing her in a boarding school for a time, but she was so distressed at the very suggestion — declaring that it would break her heart to be separated from me — that I have quite given up the idea.

"She is very bright, quick to catch an idea, and more than willing to study under my tuition, to please me, if for no other reason.

"And she has great musical talent. I must get her to sing for you all this evening. You will be delighted with her voice and her execution."

"Well, my boy, I am inclined to think she will make you happy, so far as a wife can. She is very graceful and ladylike, and I think you will succeed in educating her as far as necessary for her happiness and yours. I suppose she knows little or nothing of housewifely accomplishments, but those also she can learn. And you will live with us for the present at least, I trust, if not permanently, and if she will let me, I shall gladly teach her all I know of such matters."

"Dear mother, thank you," he said, his eyes shining with pleasure. "She could not have a more competent or kinder instructor, and I know she will be glad to avail herself of your kind offer, if only for my sake.

"She tried to learn as much as possible from good Mrs. Baird while we were there and succeeded well, too, I thought, in everything she attempted."

On leaving his mother, Rupert went in search of his wife. He found her alone in the parlor, hovering over the open piano.

"Oh, Rupert," she cried, looking up almost pleadingly into his face, "do you think I may try it? Would any one be displeased?"

"Certainly you may try it if you wish," he replied, half laughing at the absurdity of her doubt. "There is no danger of any objection being raised. But can you play on it?"

She answered only with a sportive, delighted arch smile, seated herself at the instrument, and dashed off into a brilliant waltz.

Rupert was in raptures.

"Why, Juanita!" he exclaimed, as she struck the last notes, then turned to look up into his face with dancing eyes, "you never told me you could play the piano."

"No, señor. You never asked if I could."

The different members of the family had come flocking in, drawn by the music and wondering who the player was, for the tune was new to them and the touch different from that of any of themselves.

"Give us a song, love," requested the delighted young husband.

She complied at once, and the effect upon the

small audience was fully up to Rupert's expectation. She had a magnificent voice, strong, full, of great compass and flexibility, sweet and clear as the warble of a bird, a voice that would have made her fortune as a prima donna. Nor was it entirely uncultivated.

How they crowded round her and poured out their thanks and praises, begging for another and still another till the tea bell summoned them away to their evening meal!

Juanita's playing and singing were destined henceforth to form one of the greatest enjoyments of the entire family.

Cyril came home for a short visit, and for several weeks they all (except the doctor, whose patients had to be attended to) gave themselves up, for most of the time, to the enjoyment of each other's society. It was so delightful to be together again after the long separation of Rupert and Don from the others that they seemed unable to remain apart for any length of time.

They gathered now at one of the three houses, now at another. One day the mother was the hostess, then Mildred, then Zillah. But at whichever dwelling they congregated, all were perfectly at home, Juanita very soon as much so as the rest, for they all gave her a daughter's and sister's place, calling her by those names, while the little ones were taught to say "Aunt Nita."

She was a trifle shy and reserved at first, but her timidity soon melted away under the sunshine of love that constantly shone upon her. She grew sweetly confiding and affectionate, not to her husband only but to all his relatives.

Influenced by an ardent desire to be and do all he could wish, she silently took note of all the housewifely ways of his mother and sisters, determined to copy them as nearly as possible when she also should become a housekeeper. And she rather dreading, too, the coming of the time when she must assume the duties of that position, because she felt herself hardly equal to their full performance.

It was several weeks after their arrival in Pleasant Plains that one day, finding himself alone with her, Rupert asked, "Juanita, my love, which would you prefer, going to housekeeping, or just living on here as we have been doing so far, with my father and mother?"

"Ah, Rupert, would they like to have us stay?" she asked with an eager look up into his face, for he was standing beside the low chair in which she was seated.

"Yes," he said, smiling down on her; "and I see you would like it, too."

"Oh no, not unless you please. I mean, I should prefer whatever would be most for the pleasure and happiness of my dear husband."

"Thank you, love," he said, bending down to caress her hair and cheek. "Then we will stay here at least for the present, for I perceive that will be agreeable to all parties. But whenever you weary of it, and think you would be happier in a home of your own, you must tell me so without reserve. Promise me that you will."

"Yes, señor," she said happily, "I promise. But the time will never come till I have learned to do all housewifely duties just as your dear mother does."

Her words gave him great pleasure, and she saw with delight that they did. She sprang up in a pretty, impulsive way she had, threw her arms round his neck, and gazing up into his face with eyes beaming with light and love, said, "Oh, my dear husband, how good, how kind you are to me always, always!"

"I should be brute if I were anything else to you, my precious little darling!" he said, holding her close with many a fond caress.

Rupert was again devoting himself to business with all the old energy and faithfulness.

Don, unable to decide what was best suited to his capacity and inclination, waited for some sort of opening. In the meantime, he resumed some of his former studies and spent a good deal of his leisure in the society of his sisters and Dr. Landreth's relative and guest, Miss Flora Weston.

He was pleased with her, and the liking was mutual. Don was a handsome, high-spirited fellow and could be very entertaining in conversation. And Flora, with improving health and spirits, had become quite an attractive girl.

The friendship at length ripened into love. She remained in Pleasant Plains through the winter, and before spring had fairly opened, the two were affianced, with the knowledge and consent of parents and relatives on both sides. But as both were very young, the marriage would not take place for a year or more.

In May, Mr. Weston came for his daughter.

His home was in New Jersey, where he was largely engaged in manufacturing, and he had not been long in Pleasant Plains before he proposed that Don should take a position in his business establishment, with the prospect of becoming a partner at no very distant day.

Don thanked him heartily, took a few days to consider the matter and consult with parents and friends, then accepted the offer and again bade farewell to home and kindred. But this time the parting was by no means so sorrowful as on a former occasion.

He was not going so far away or into such dangers, difficulties, and temptations, and might hope to return now and then for a visit to his childhood home. It was but such a separation as is common between parents and their sons grown to man's estate.

Here we will leave our friends for the present, perhaps taking up the thread of our narrative again at some future day and telling what befell them in later years.

THE END

The Original Elsie Classics